Blame It On The Carols

Samantha Baca

Sugarplum Falls Series

Blame It On The Mistletoe

Blame It On The Eggnog

Blame It On The Candy Canes

Blame It On The Blizzard

Blame It On The Reindeer

Blame It On The Carols

Blame It On The Lattes

Blame It On The Secret Santa

Cover Design: Richard Baca
Image (s): DepositPhotos

Contents

One
Aiden

"We're closed for the night," I hollered as the door opened, letting in a gust of cold air. I continued wiping down the counter, expecting whoever it was to leave. Instead, my body tensed as I heard the familiar sound of heels as they headed my way. I swallowed hard and looked up, not believing my eyes.

"What are you doing here, Makayla?" I asked, taking a step away from the bar as she got closer.

"Hi, Aiden." She held her hands tightly in front of her as if she was as nervous to see me as I was to see her.

It had been six years, but not much had changed. Her long blond hair hung loosely in a low ponytail as bangs framed her face, showing off her sparkling blue eyes. She still looked like the girl I fell in love with in high school, only more grown up.

"What are you doing here?" I asked again, trying to keep any hint of emotion out of my voice. I hadn't talked to Makayla since she walked out of my life and never looked back.

"I'm in town for a few weeks," she said softly, seeming unsure of how to talk to me. At least the feeling was mutual. "My mom is part of the Sugarplum Falls choir and they have the annual caroling competition coming up."

I nodded, knowing all about the caroling competition and how this year it was an even bigger deal because they were trying to win it so they could use the prize money to do repairs at the church.

"Well, I'm sure your mom will be happy to see you."

I lowered my eyes, but not before I noticed the disappointed look on her face.

"What about you? Are you not happy to see me?" she questioned.

My pulse raced as I struggled with what to say.

"I don't know," I answered honestly, finally lifting my face to look at her.

"That's fair, I guess." She shifted her weight and nodded.

"We haven't talked in over six years, Makayla. Then you just show up out of the blue…" I held my hands in front of me. "I don't know what you want me to say."

She sighed heavily, her chest rising and falling as she let out her breath.

"I don't know, Aiden. I guess maybe I was just hoping we could move past what happened all those years ago and start over fresh?"

"You broke my heart!" I nearly shouted, slamming my hands on the counter. "It's not that easy to just wash it all away and pretend it never happened. *You* walked away and didn't bother to look back as I struggled to put the pieces of my life back together. You don't get to waltz in here like nothing happened and expect that I'm going to be happy to see you."

She lowered her head and nodded.

"You're right. I'm sorry. It was a mistake to come here."

She turned and walked out, the door slamming shut behind her. I scrubbed a hand down my face, not believing what just happened.

Two
Makayla

I cried on the short drive from Sugar Faced Bar to my mom's house, trying to get myself together before she saw me. I hadn't told her about my little detour because I wanted to be the one to tell Aiden I was back in town. The last thing I wanted was for him to find out about it through the local gossip mill. I had been gone from Sugarplum Falls long enough not to miss that anymore, but I still knew it was important to keep my head down and stay out of it if possible.

I pulled into the driveway and wiped my eyes one final time. It was pointless to act like nothing was wrong because my mom always had a way of seeing right through me. She would know that I had been crying, and she would likely guess it was because I had gone to see Aiden. She wasn't stupid, and if anything, she was the only person who knew how devastated and heartbroken I was when I left six years ago.

After I grabbed my suitcase from the trunk, I made my way to the door, not at all surprised that she was standing there waiting for me. Her arms were open as I fell into them, allowing her to hug and comfort me the way I needed.

"Give him time to come around," she said gently while rubbing my back. "I'm sure he was a little blindsided by everything, and you know how that can make people defensive."

I nodded and pulled away, wiping my eyes again.

"Welcome home, sugar. Come on inside before you catch a cold."

She stepped to the side and grabbed my suitcase before closing the door.

Everything in the house was the same way it had been when I lived here. Not much had changed other than a few new pictures that were added to the mantle of my mom and her new boyfriend. They had been dating for a little over a year, but this was the first time I was going to meet him.

Life had been busy and nonstop, which meant I didn't get to come home as often as I wanted. That also meant that my mom moved on with her life while I was out living mine. She and my dad got a divorce when I was in middle school, but she never allowed herself to date anyone until after I left home.

"How was your flight?" she asked, tucking my suitcase beneath the island in the kitchen as she put the kettle on the stove and turned it on. It didn't matter how late it was; there was always time for tea, according to my mom.

"It was good. Long. But thankfully not too full since it was such a late flight."

"That's good. Brock checked the road conditions several times before you landed. He was ready to get the truck loaded so he could go get you. We didn't know what kind of rental car they were going to give you, and he didn't trust it would be good enough to get you here safely."

I smiled, loving the way her eyes lit up as she talked about him.

"That was very sweet of him," I said, sitting on one of the barstools while she grabbed the tea packets. "Where is he?"

"He had to go to work for a few hours. They had a doctor call in sick, so he's covering in the ER tonight. I thought maybe we could all do lunch together this weekend?"

"Sure, that sounds wonderful."

My mom smiled and squeezed my hand, something I hadn't realized how much I missed until now.

Three
Aiden

"I can help you here," Victor said, smiling as he stood behind the register. I was expecting Sam to be there this morning but was too tired from not sleeping last night to worry about it. I could catch up with him later.

"Thanks. Can I get a large black eye?"

"Woah. Sounds like someone had a rough night," Sam said, coming around the corner. I knew Victor had worked with him for a few weeks now, but I couldn't help but laugh at the shocked and confused look on his face as he tried to figure out what I had ordered.

"Something like that," I mumbled, running a hand through my short hair.

"It's coffee black with two shots of espresso," he explained to Victor as he set a stack of napkins down on the counter behind them. "What's up? You seem off."

I stepped to the side and out of earshot of Victor and the other customers as Sam followed me to the end of the counter.

"Makayla showed up last night."

Sam's eyes widened as he folded his arms over his chest.

"As in your *ex*-girlfriend, Makayla?"

"The one and only."

"The one who broke your heart and moved to LA to start a music career?"

"Yup."

"The one who has won several awards, including album of the year?"

I tilted my head and leveled him with a look. He knew damn well who I was talking about.

"Wow. I don't know what to say. What did she want?"

"Honestly? I have no idea. She said she's in town because of her mom and the caroling competition, but I didn't ask questions."

"That's crazy. Did she say how long she'll be here?"

"A few weeks."

"How do you feel about that?"

I shrugged and took the cup Victor handed to me.

"I don't know. It kept me up last night knowing she was back in town. It was like she had already gotten under my skin, and we weren't even around each other for more than ten minutes. I couldn't stop thinking about the last time I saw her, and we all know how that went."

"Maybe that's a sign," Sam said, cocking his head to look at me.

"A sign about what?"

"That the universe is bringing you two back together for a reason. If she's already getting under your skin, maybe that means you never really got over her. And if you still have feelings for her, this could be your chance to act on them. To tell her how you really feel."

"I appreciate your delusion with this," I said sarcastically. "But it's not like that with Makayla. Even if I still had feelings for her, she wouldn't be willing to put her life on hold to be with me. Nor would I ask her to. That's why we didn't work out the first time and why things won't work out for us now. Our lives and what we want are too different."

"Don't be so sure about that," Sam warned with a grin.

I rolled my eyes and tried to fight the corners of my lips as they turned upward—not because I found any humor in this, but because I was exhausted and his smile felt contagious.

"You can be a hopeless romantic all day if you want. But some of us live in the real world, which means we have shit to do. And that does *not* involve trying to reconcile broken things from our past." I tapped the counter with my knuckles and stepped away. "I'll see you tonight. It's karaoke night, so come prepared."

"Alright, but only if you sing with me."

"You're my best friend, but there ain't no way in hell you're getting me on stage to sing." I raised my eyebrows at him and pointed a finger.

"We'll see about that."

By the time I finished running errands and got to the bar,

Jackie was already there. She was the assistant manager and had been working for me for years, which meant she was a godsend for me on days like today when my mind was scattered. She would somehow just know to take charge and get things done without me having to be present.

"Hey, how's it going?" she asked when I walked in.

"Fine," I answered with a heavy sigh. I didn't want to keep talking about Makayla, but I felt the stares from people in town as they whispered about how they'd heard she was back. It wasn't like it was a big surprise that we had strong feelings about each other, given we had been high school sweethearts and the whole town assumed we would get married and start a family with the way things were going between us.

"There's a fresh pot of coffee ready and I ordered lunch. It should be here in half an hour or so."

I arched an eyebrow and caught her eye.

"What?" She lifted her hands in the air helplessly. "You look like shit for one, and two, the gossip mill has already started. I just thought food and caffeine might be a good way for you to get your night started since you know people are going to ask if you've talked to Makayla yet. I just wanted to get as far ahead of it as I could and maybe make your night a little easier."

"I look like shit? Gee, thanks."

"You know what I mean," she replied with a laugh. "I'm not saying you won't still have women throwing themselves at you after a few rounds. Just that I can see the dark circles under your eyes from here."

"Maybe I should wear sunglasses and hide in the back?"

"No can do. You're running the karaoke tonight."

"Since when?" I frowned as I stepped behind the bar to pour myself a cup of coffee—not that I wasn't already over-caffeinated as it was.

"Since Justin called in sick. I'll cover the bar, and you can deal with the drunk women who think they can sing."

"Why don't I handle the bar, and you take over karaoke?"

"Because, you know no one does it when I try to run it. People look forward to interacting with you. It'll go so much better if you do it."

I rolled my eyes and took a sip, allowing the hot liquid to burn down my throat.

Four
Makayla

"This is a terrible idea," I hissed as my mom locked her arm in mine and practically dragged me through the parking lot.

"No, it's not."

"Yes, it is," I insisted. "Aiden does *not* want to see me. I don't know why you would think it was a good idea to come here tonight when he clearly said he wasn't excited that I was back in town."

"Yeah, well, people change. Besides, it's not about Aiden tonight." She stopped and looked me square in the eyes as we stood outside the door. I could hear the bass as the music blared inside.

"Seriously?" I tilted my head to the side, calling her on her bullshit.

"Seriously. I don't care about what he thinks or how upset he might be having you here tonight. We only have a few weeks until the caroling competition, which means we need to squeeze in as much practice as possible. The rest of the group is meeting here tonight, and we're going to get up there every chance we get. Since you're taking over Brenda's spot, we need to make sure you're ready. The only way to do that is to rehearse as much as possible."

"You do know that I sing for a living, right?" I teased with a wink. "I have a few albums out and have been on tour for the last ten months, traveling the world and performing for people who pay to see me. Oh, and I've won an award or two." I gave her my biggest grin and ducked as she swatted at me.

"Yes, you smart ass. But singing on stage by yourself is different than singing with a choir. Plus, this is soulful Christmas music. You can't be popping your hips out or trying to grind while you sing songs about Jesus." She pointed a finger at me, which only prompted me to lean forward to try to bite it.

She shook her head and sighed before pulling the door open.

I stepped inside, feeling the knot in my stomach grow harder as I quickly scanned the room, looking for Aiden.

"Over there," my mom said, pointing to a large table in the corner.

I followed her lead, keeping my head down as I tucked a strand of hair behind my ear. I had debated pulling it up but decided that it looked better down—not that I was trying to impress anyone. Keyword: Aiden.

He didn't care that I was back in town, so why would he care what I looked like? I could come in wearing a garbage bag and have maggots in my hair, and he would be just as unimpressed to see me as he was last night.

I took a seat in the back, hoping to hide in the shadows while my mom took her time saying hi to everyone. It wasn't like they didn't see each other a few times a week, but it was still nice to see her with her friends.

I picked up one of the menus from the table and held it in front of my face while my mom started waving someone over to the table. I knew it was Aiden before I saw him because my body immediately began buzzing with electricity the way it used to.

"Hello, ladies. Nice to see you again. You all here for karaoke?" he asked, his voice unusually calm, which meant he hadn't seen me yet.

"Yes, we thought we could use the time to get in a few more rehearsals before the big competition," my mother said, reaching over to lower the menu from in front of me. "Makayla is taking Brenda's place since she's recovering from surgery for the next few weeks. We want to make sure she has time to learn the songs before then."

I slowly looked up to find green eyes locked on me. He rubbed his lips together, his jaw incredibly tight as he clenched it. His hair was shorter than it was when I saw him last night and I couldn't help but wonder if he had gotten a haircut this morning, knowing how I used to prefer it short like it is now.

"Well, Ashley will be over soon to take your drink orders. I'll bring over the songbook and request forms so you can get yours in. Karaoke will start in twenty minutes."

"Thank you. Should we place our food order with Ashley, or can we give it to you now?" my mother pressed, keeping him there longer. I knew what she was doing just as much as Aiden did, yet being from a small town, he smiled and appeased her because that's what people in small towns did. They were friendly, even when they didn't want to be.

I could feel the tension radiating from his body as he pulled a notepad from his back pocket.

"I can take the food order," he said, his smile tight as if it pained him to be there. "What can I get you ladies?"

They started at the other end of the table, making their way around until I was last. I shook my head, trying not to pull anyone's attention to me as I declined to order.

"You need to eat, Makayla," my mother insisted. "She'll have the—"

"Cheeseburger and fries, no salt, extra cheese," Aiden said, meeting my eyes again.

My heart fluttered in my chest, making me squirm in my seat from the overwhelming emotions that were threatening to take over me. Of course he knew my order. At one point, Aiden knew everything about me, and that was something I used to take comfort in.

I nodded and looked away, not bothering to watch as he walked off.

Five
Aiden

"Here's the order for table five. Make sure the burger is well done, no pink." I added the ticket to the line and made sure the kitchen staff heard me before I went behind the bar to get their drinks. Everyone had ordered a cocktail or a glass of wine except for Makayla. She didn't bother to ask for anything, which bothered me. I knew I hadn't been very welcoming when she came in to see me last night, but I was caught off guard. It was still hard to see her because so much had changed between us, but my heart refused to accept that as it clung to the tiny thread of hope that things could be different between us.

I got the drinks situated on the tray and then filled a glass with ice water for Makayla. I knew that she used to be a beer and burger kind of girl back when we were dating, but who knew if she still liked it? Why would I expect to know anything about her now? I'd taken a guess on her food order, but she hadn't stopped to correct me, which made me think maybe things hadn't changed as much as I thought.

I made my way through the tables that were starting to fill up and set the drinks down on the empty table beside me. The ladies were all laughing at something her mom, Jill, had said, but I noticed that Makayla seemed off in her own world. She was chewing her nails and staring down at the table, something that made my heart hurt for her.

I passed the drinks around, then excused myself as I headed back behind the bar. It was a risky move, but I found myself doing it anyway as I prepared a special cocktail for Makayla. I may not have been ecstatic to see her, but that didn't mean that I ever stopped caring about her. It was just a shock that she was back in town, and it took me a little longer than expected to warm up to the idea. Mainly because I didn't want to get my hopes up that things would be the same between us as they were before she left.

The ladies were all sipping on their drinks as Makayla swirled her straw in circles, pushing the ice through the water.

"Dirty Reindeer Balls," I said, clearing my throat to get Makayla to look at me as I extended the glass to her.

"I'm sorry?" she stammered, looking confused as her cheeks flushed the prettiest shade of red. "Oh, no. I didn't order a drink."

"I know. It's on the house."

She opened her mouth to respond, then snapped it closed as she took the drink. The older women talked behind their hands, likely commenting on how vulgar the name of the drink was, though they all had smiles on their faces. Then Makayla smiled for the first time since I'd seen her, and that smile alone started shattering the steel wall I'd built around my heart.

The night moved quickly, and before I knew it, the bar was packed. The tables were completely full, and every seat at the bar was occupied. It was standing room only and close to getting shut down by the fire marshal for exceeding the occupancy limit if we didn't stop allowing people in. It always sucked having to turn people away, but it was also a good problem to have because our bar sales were usually high when we were this busy.

Karaoke was always a big hit, but it seemed to be even more popular the closer we got to Christmas. It was like everyone was coming in to have a drink or two and relax for a bit. I didn't blame them; it was crazy this time of year and I didn't even have family in town to buy for, let alone kids. I couldn't imagine the stress parents were under to make the magic of Christmas happen for their little ones. Between taking them to see Santa and sneaking around to buy presents that he would leave on Christmas Eve, it felt like too much.

"Alright, next up, we have the Sugarplum Sweethearts," I announced, making sure the microphone was loud enough to be heard over the crowd of people talking around me. "Come on up, ladies."

There was a makeshift stage at the front of the bar that we used for karaoke and it worked perfectly. The ladies all made their way over, and I noticed Makayla staying behind as she nursed her drink. Her mom bent down to say something, but Makayla shook her head.

"It looks like we've got the full team tonight, folks. Get ready for a real Christmas treat as we have Makayla Hendrix in the house with us," I added, noticing the way her head immediately shot up, eyes glaring at me.

Her mother gave her another nudge, and Makayla reluctantly stood up. The crowd began cheering and clapping as they all made their way to the stage. I tried not to watch as Makayla walked in front of me, her round ass drawing my attention in the skin-tight jeans she was wearing. She was curvy when we dated, but never like this.

I forced myself to ignore the thoughts that wanted to infiltrate my mind as she took her place on the stage behind the other women until her mom forced her to the front. Now wasn't the time to entertain dirty thoughts about what it would be like to be with her again. That would have to wait until later when I was home by myself. Or better yet— never. It wasn't like there would be anything happening between us. That ship had sailed.

I pressed a few buttons and waited for the music to start. They were singing Silent Night, and I had heard them do it a few times already, as they came in often to rehearse. But this would be the first time I'd heard Makayla sing in person since she left.

<u>Six</u>
Makayla

I didn't know if it was from whatever was in the Dirty Reindeer Balls drink that Aiden had made for me or if it was the way he was watching me from the DJ podium, but suddenly—I had the courage I needed to take the stage and sing. It wasn't like I didn't do this for a living. But the difference was that I knew these people. I knew Aiden. And I'd never performed for the people in the small town I left behind when I started my career.

The ladies all stood behind me, and it felt weird that we hadn't talked about what we would do or how this would work. My mom assured me that I just needed to sing, and they would do the rest—which didn't really sound that promising. I had worked with plenty of backup singers in my life, and they always needed guidance, no matter how experienced they were.

I took a deep breath, pulled my shoulders back, and closed my eyes as I began singing. Silent Night was my favorite song, and I had sung it so many times as a child that I knew every single word. I was so lost in the moment that I hadn't even noticed how perfectly the women were harmonizing behind me as they sang along. I knew they were good and had won the caroling competition a few times, but I had no idea they were *that* good. That was what happened when you moved away and didn't make time for those you left behind—you missed out on all of the good things that happened without you.

I continued singing, completely caught up in the song, as I slowly opened my eyes and found Aiden watching me. His arms were folded over his chest, and his body looked rigid. But his attention was solely on me. I looked into his eyes as I kept singing, holding onto this feeling before it ended. It was hard to describe what it was, but I knew I had never felt anything like it before. It was a mix of acknowledging what we used to have while also being curious about what could be between us if given a chance.

Once the song was over, the ladies quickly cleared off the stage and left me to return the microphone to Aiden. He had already started another song to fill the space before he called the next person up for karaoke, which meant I couldn't just shove it at him and run off like I wanted to.

"Here you go," I said, handing him the microphone.

His fingers brushed mine as he took it, a surge of electricity washing over my skin from the contact.

"You did amazing up there," he said softly, not looking at me as he set it down next to the others.

"Thank you." My cheeks flamed as a blush crept across them. I turned to go back to my seat but stopped when I felt his hand on my arm.

"I didn't mean what I said last night," he said, his tone firm.

I looked away before looking at him, unsure of what to say.

"It's okay if you did," I admitted. "I knew that things between us would be different when I came back. I don't blame you for being upset with me or for being caught off guard with me just showing up out of the blue."

"I was definitely caught off guard." He smiled and I looked away because I couldn't handle what it did to my heart.

"Well, I'm sorry about that."

"You don't need to keep apologizing for coming back. Your mom is still here, and you have every right to visit her. I'm sorry that I wasn't more welcoming. I'm sure the town is more than excited to have a local celebrity here."

The town—not him.

"Thanks. It's nice being back. I'd better get over there before they sign us up for more songs," I joked, not knowing what else to say.

"I wouldn't worry yourself too much with that."

"Why not?"

He held up a stack of papers and shook them in the air.

"Because they've already signed up for all of these. Looks like you guys will be here for a while."

I sighed heavily, knowing it was going to be a long night made even harder knowing that I would be stuck having to fight whatever these feelings were that I was getting every time I looked at Aiden. I was only supposed to stay in Sugarplum Falls for a few weeks, which meant I had no time to fall in love again.

26

Seven
Aiden

It was hard being around Makayla and not touching her like I wanted to. It wasn't my fault that my body refused to forget the insane chemistry we had or that every time she walked past me, I smelled the familiar scent of the coconut shampoo she used. Her heart had imprinted on mine long ago, and there was nothing I could do about that.

After we closed for the night, I sent Jackie home while I finished up. There wasn't much to do since she'd already had the kitchen crew clean up and prep for tomorrow. But still, I needed to keep myself busy so my mind would stay off of Makayla.

"What else do you need help with?" Sam asked, carrying the cleaning stuff he'd used to wipe down the tables. I'd told him he didn't need to stick around since it was so late and he had an early day tomorrow. He was supposed to *sell* the lattes, not drink all of them.

"I think that's it. I'm just closing out the register, and then I'll be done."

"Cool. I'll hang out for a few then."

I looked over my shoulder as he sat on the barstool and folded his hands in front of him on the counter.

"Don't you need to get some sleep? You're going to be struggling in the morning if you try to pull an all-nighter. We're not in our twenties anymore," I teased.

"You act like we're old." He rolled his eyes. "You just barely turned thirty a few months ago, and I'm only thirty-five. We still have plenty of youth in us."

"Yeah, but you're already yawning," I pointed out as he tried to hide it behind his hand. "You have work tomorrow, while I don't have to be back until tomorrow evening. I don't want you to be exhausted because of me."

"I'm fine," he said, waving dismissively. "Besides, Mary is opening tomorrow. I don't have to be in until the afternoon. We have a few new hires, so I'm going in to show them around, and then we'll do some of their training after we close."

"You guys have had a lot of new hires lately. Why aren't any of them working out?"

He shrugged and leaned his head back on his shoulders.

"I don't know. I guess a lot of them are still young and don't really want to work. Most of them have been high school kids, and we all know how that goes. No one likes to get up that early to come to work, and in my line of business, our day starts before the rooster crows."

I nodded because I knew how that went. I'd gone through the same thing a few months ago looking for bussers to help clean up with the evening crowd. It was light work, mainly clearing the tables and washing dishes, but no one wanted to do it.

It was quiet for a few minutes while I finished closing out

the register. I stuffed the cash and the paperwork into the money bag and then put it in the safe so Jackie could take it to the bank in the morning.

"You ready to go?" I asked, pulling my keys out of my pocket so I could lock up.

As we headed out into the cold, Sam stopped and stared at me.

"I know you don't want to hear it, but I'm going to say it anyway."

I pulled my shoulders back and waited.

"Makayla still looks at you the same way she did six years ago."

My heart plummeted in my chest because as much as I wanted his words to be true, I knew that they weren't.

"We're just friends," I lied, mainly because I wasn't sure you could even call us friends at this point.

He shrugged and shoved his hands in his pockets as we headed toward our vehicles.

"I'm just saying, you didn't see how she looked at you when she thought you weren't looking. I know that look, Aiden. And I know you well enough to know that you're going to do everything in your power to avoid allowing yourself to see it. But I wouldn't be me if I didn't come to you, offering you some sage advice and shit," he teased, nudging my arm with his.

"Part of me wishes that were true," I admitted, glancing at him over my shoulder. "I miss her. Having her here has been a harsh reminder of what I lost. But the fact remains that I can't give her what she wants. It doesn't matter whether I still love her because deep down, I know that what she loves isn't me."

Eight
Makayla

"Last night went well," my mom said, pouring herself a cup of coffee while I sipped mine at the island. I'd gotten up a few minutes before her, mainly because I couldn't sleep thinking about Aiden. He had been on my mind so much last night that I found myself wanting to hump my pillow to get rid of the building tension I felt between my thighs every time I pictured his stupid dimpled smile.

"It did," I agreed. "You guys have really mastered the songs. I think maybe a few more rehearsals as we get closer to the competition will help, but other than that, we are good to go."

"I reached out to Aiden this morning, and he agreed to let us use the stage at the bar before they open so we can keep practicing. The girls can all meet there around one this afternoon, but I thought it might be good if you and I got there a little early. Then you could get some solo practice in."

My mouth hung open as I stared at her in disbelief. Was she serious right now? It was hard enough being around Aiden in a room full of people, but spending a few hours there with hardly anyone else around would be pure torture.

"Are you kidding me?"

"What?" she asked, trying to hide her grin behind her

coffee mug as she took a sip. "A little practice won't kill you, Makayla."

No, but being around Aiden and not being able to jump his bones might.

"What's wrong with rehearsing at the church?" I questioned, setting my cup on the island and resting my hands in front of me to keep from fidgeting. "You guys literally sing there every single Sunday during the services. I don't see why we can't just go there."

"Because they're currently working on repairing the roof. There would be too much noise and lots of distractions. It's better to do it at the bar, and since they won't be open yet, we don't have to worry about bothering anyone other than Aiden."

"Yeah, 'cause I'm sure this isn't going to *bother* him at all," I replied with a bit too much sarcasm.

"He already said it was fine. I don't know what you're making such a big deal about." She huffed and threw her hand in the air as she took another drink.

"Oh, I'm sure he was just being nice, Mom. It's what people in small towns do. Even if he had a problem with it, he wouldn't tell you. He would just smile and say okay."

"You're right. And since you're back home, in a *small town*, it wouldn't hurt you to be nice to Aiden."

I didn't think it was possible, but my jaw dropped even further.

"What are you talking about? I haven't been mean to him."

"Not necessarily, but you've been distant. He went out of

his way to make sure you had dinner last night *and* took the initiative to get you something to drink. I know you guys have a complicated past, but that doesn't mean you have to let it ruin your future."

"You say *future* as if that's even a possibility for us."

The words were out of my mouth before I could even second-guess them.

"Who knows, maybe there will be. A little *Christmas miracle*, if you will." She winked and set her cup down. "Now go get ready, or we're going to be late."

I glanced up at the clock on the wall, frowning.

"It's barely nine in the morning. I thought you said the girls weren't going to be there until one?"

"Yes, and I also said that I thought it would be good for you to get some practice time by yourself."

"Four hours? I think that's a bit excessive, don't you?"

"Nope. By the time you take a shower and get ready, it'll be close to ten. And, of course, I always have to stop by Sugarplum Lattes, so that adds more time. Three hours should be good, but we gotta get a move on it. Chop chop, let's get going."

She snapped her fingers as she walked out of the kitchen, leaving me wondering why I agreed to come back and do this in the first place.

****

My foot tapped anxiously on the tile floor as we stood in line at Sugarplum Lattes. My mother had insisted on coming inside to place an order, even though there was no one in the drive-through. It wasn't that I was overly eager or excited to go see Aiden, but I also just wanted to get it over with.

"I can help you here," Sam called, smiling as we approached. "What can I get for you ladies this morning?"

"I will do the gingerbread latte," my mother answered, sliding her credit card out of her wallet while waiting for me to tell him what I wanted.

"Surprise me," I said, already feeling overwhelmed and anxious.

"Do you still like peppermint?" he asked, watching me carefully.

"Yes," I replied slowly, unsure of how he remembered that. "How did you know that?"

"It's a gift." He shrugged as he added my drink to the order. "It'll be ready in a few minutes."

We stepped to the side as my mom put her card back into her wallet.

"Do you mind waiting for the drinks? I want to pop over to Sugarplum Sweets to see if Andi has any truffles ready yet this morning."

Before I could agree, she rushed out the door and left me there to wait for our drinks by myself.

A few minutes later, Sam called my name, likely having seen that my mom had left.

"Thank you," I said, grabbing the two large cups from him.

"No problem."

I was about to turn and leave when he stopped me.

"Hey, would you mind taking this one to Aiden for me? He texted me that he wasn't going to be able to make it in after all, and since you're heading that way, I thought maybe you could deliver it for me?" His eyes pleaded as mine narrowed, wondering what he was up to.

"How did you know I was headed there?"

"It's a small town," he answered with a cheeky smile as he grabbed a drink tray and loaded all three in for me before adding a few candy canes as well. "Everyone knows everything in a small town. Enjoy the latte."

"Thank you. Are the candy canes for Aiden?" I asked, not wanting to mess up whatever he had ordered.

"There's one for each of you."

I raised an eyebrow at him, wondering if he was trying to recreate that scene from Lady and The Tramp where they share the same noodle in the spaghetti. Things weren't like that with Aiden, and at this rate, he would be lucky if there was still a candy cane left for him by the time I got there. Stress eating was a real thing, and I was beyond out of sorts this morning.

36

Nine
Aiden

I was an idiot for agreeing to allow Jill to use the stage at the bar for rehearsals. I knew she was just doing it to force me and Makayla to spend more time together. There was nothing wrong with the church, which was where the ladies usually practiced. They had only recently started coming to karaoke night to get some extra sessions in there, but even then, it wasn't like you could really call it rehearsal when they had to share the time with everyone else who wanted to sing.

I was in the back when I heard the front door open and stiffened, not sure if I was ready to see her again. I had tried to force myself to accept that I would see her while she was in town, but I hadn't quite expected to see so much of her so soon.

"Hey," I said, shoving my hands in my pockets as I attempted to smile at Makayla and her mom.

"Hi, Aiden," Jill cooed, coming in to give me a hug. "Thank you again for letting us do this. It means so much to the ladies that we can squeeze in some extra rehearsal time with Makayla before the big event."

"Not a problem," I said, only half lying. It wouldn't be a problem under any other circumstances, but given that it was forcing me and Makayla to spend more time together, it felt like one.

"This is from Sam," Makayla said, extending one of the to-go cups in her hand to me as her mom lifted her phone and held it up for us to see before walking off to take a call.

"Thank you." I tried not to frown but was confused as to why Sam would send her with a drink for me, especially when I hadn't ordered anything. Not only that, he knew I didn't drink the fancy lattes he made because I preferred my coffee black. Yet this was a peppermint mocha, something I never drank.

Makayla watched me as I pulled the stick out that was keeping it from spilling and took a sip. Her eyebrows rose as she waited for my reaction.

I turned my head and coughed, shaking my head to clear the sweetness overload that was overpowering my tongue.

"Not a fan?" she asked, head cocked to the side as she continued studying me.

I shook my head and wiped my mouth.

"Not really."

"Then why did you order it?"

"I didn't." I set it on the counter behind me and watched as her lips parted slowly to take a sip of hers.

"Really? That's weird." She continued to frown as Jill made her way over to us, clutching her phone to her chest.

"I'm so sorry, but I need to leave for a bit. Shirley fell in the tub, and I need to go see if she's okay. I might need to take her to the hospital. I'll be back around two with the girls."

"I thought Shirley just got her bathroom redone and had a walk-in shower installed?" I questioned, both Makayla and I watching as Jill blushed profusely.

"Oh. Yes. You're right. She must have meant that she fell in the shower."

"I thought you said the girls were coming at one, not two?" Makayla asked, pinning her mom with a look.

"Umm. I got a message that Susie needed a little more time to feed her fish. You know how squirrely and demanding they can be." Jill laughed nervously, her eyes widening so big that they started to scare me. "Best to let her deal with that, and then we can rehearse later. Okay. I've got to go. Be back later. Bye!"

She rushed out the door before either of us could say anything.

"Was that weird to you too?" I asked, scrubbing a hand down the scruff dotting my jawline.

"Yup. Just as weird as Sam insisting that he was sending me with an order *you* placed but were unable to come get it. And on top of that, it wasn't even a drink you like."

"Gotta love small towns and meddling people," I said with a heavy sigh, tilting my head back on my neck.

"Indeed. But on the plus side, Sam sent over two candy canes and said we had to share them." She handed me one, and I shook my head, knowing exactly what that fucker was up to. Sam was definitely going to hear about this.

"What?" she asked with a nervous laugh as I took it. "Are they poisoned or something?"

"No, not at all. Sam has this thing he does with the candy canes," I explained, taking hers and setting it on the bar top beside mine. "If you put them together, they make a heart."

"Oh." She rubbed her lips together as we both stared at them. "Well, that's very convenient, isn't it?"

"It seems we're being set up, whether we like it or not."

Ten
Makayla

"I'll call a cab and get out of your hair," I offered, not sure what to do with myself now that my mom conveniently bailed on me.

"You don't need to do that."

"Aiden, I'm not going to make you uncomfortable by having me here. I can come back later with the rest of the girls *if* that's even still the plan. I swear, I've never been lied to as much as I have this morning by my mom."

"You don't make me uncomfortable," he said, though I could see the way his body stiffened as he said it.

"You don't have to be nice or pretend that you're okay with this," I replied with a heavy sigh. "I get that things between us have changed. I don't know how to fix that, or if we even can, but I do know that my leaving will give you some space so we don't have to pretend like things are fine between us."

I turned to leave, startled when his hand reached out and grabbed my wrist. He pulled me into him, and suddenly, all of the tension that had been lingering between us faded away. My body melted against his, missing the way it felt next to mine.

"Some things will *never* change between us, Mak," he said softly, lifting my chin with his finger so I had to look up at him.

Then, without any warning, his lips were on mine, and my fingers were wrapped tightly in his hair as the kiss intensified. It didn't matter how much time had passed; our bodies knew each other and acted as if nothing had changed.

I moaned against this mouth, that yearning feeling building between my legs again. His hands slid down my waist and grabbed my ass, lifting me to his hips as he backed us up against the low counter behind the bar.

"Fuck, Mak," he breathed, my name sounding sinful coming off his tongue. "Do you have any idea what you're doing to me?"

I reached down and cupped my hand over his erection, grinning when I realized how affected he was by this as well.

"It seems our bodies haven't forgotten how much they like each other," I offered, leaning my head to the side as he kissed my neck. A shiver ran through me as my nipples hardened beneath the lace fabric of my bra.

"Not even a little bit." He growled as he gripped my ass harder, his need for more matching my own.

"Hey, it's just me," a female voice called, startling us as we quickly separated.

I wiped at my mouth, turning away from her as Aiden shifted out from in front of me.

"Hey, Jackie," he said, sounding way too out of breath to pretend we weren't doing anything.

"Oh my God," she shrieked. "I'm so sorry. I didn't know there was anyone else here. I just saw your truck was here, and you always come in early—"

"It's fine."

"No. No. I'm gonna go. I'll just come back later," she insisted.

I tried to keep from looking back at her because I didn't want her to see the embarrassment on my face from being caught. I could only imagine what would have happened had we not been.

Just then, my phone started ringing.

Perfect time for a distraction.

"Hey, Curtis. What's up?" I answered, twirling a strand of hair around my finger while ignoring the conversation Aiden was having behind me.

"Where are you?"

His voice sounded panicked, which immediately made me feel panicked.

"I'm in Sugarplum Falls. Remember, I told you I was coming here to spend time with my mom and do that caroling competition?"

"Shit." He exhaled heavily on the other line. "How big is the town you're in?"

"I don't know," I replied, trying to keep myself calm. "It's not big by any means. Why? What's going on? You're starting to freak me out."

I wasn't sure if it was the tone of my voice or my words that grabbed Aiden and Jackie's attention, but it was now on me.

"We got a few packages delivered to you today. I went ahead and opened them, and...."

I raised my eyebrows, sitting on pins and needles while I waited for him to spit it out.

"And?" I prompted.

"It's bad."

"Curtis, you're killing me here. Just tell me what's going on."

"I don't want to freak you out, but it seems Kevin is back."

"Are you kidding me?"

"I wish I was. The packages have lingerie and *toys* inside them, but I think it's definitely him. We also checked your PO box, and there were a handful of letters, all from him."

I puffed my cheeks full of air and slowly let it out. This was not the news I wanted to get.

"Fuck."

"Yeah, fuck is right," he agreed. "Send me the info on where you're staying, and I'll send a security team your way. We already know this guy is crazy. I don't think we should risk your safety right now. Especially in a small town with few places to hide you."

"I'm staying with my mom," I whispered, immediately hating that I was now putting her life in danger. "Shit."

"What's going on," Aiden asked, gently touching my elbow to get my attention. His eyes were locked on me, worry evident by the way his brow creased in concern.

"Hold on for a second, Curtis. I'm going to put you on speakerphone."

"Okay. Are you trying to set me up with someone? I mean, I'm not opposed to small-town life, but I could get on board if he's cute. Is he cute?"

"Oh my God," I said with a laugh, which felt good given the way my blood pressure had spiked from the worry he'd created. "Stop being ridiculous. I'm at my friend Aiden's bar, so I'm going to put you on speakerphone so we can figure out the next step."

"Aiden, as in the guy you've been desperately in love with since the day I met you?" he asked the second I turned the speakerphone on. I closed my eyes and winced—*and now such unfortunate timing.*

"Aiden, this is Curtis, my manager. Curtis, this is Aiden," I said through gritted teeth, feeling the heat of Aiden's gaze on my face. I knew my cheeks were flushed with heat, but it wasn't like I could try to deny anything after what had just happened between Aiden and me.

"Nice to meet you," Curtis said. "And since it seems I'm not your type, I'll get straight to it. Makayla has had a stalker for at least six months now, and we got packages delivered to the studio for her today. When I checked her PO box, I saw a stack of letters he'd sent as well. I know that she's planning to spend Christmas in Sugarplum Falls, but I would feel better if I sent a security team down to watch over her."

"A stalker?" Aiden questioned, looking directly at me as I let out a shuddered breath.

"It's a long story," I said, dismissing the look he gave me. "I don't know that it would be the best idea to send a team here, Curtis. We've seen how much attention they draw when I go on vacation. I can only imagine what would happen if they tried to blend into a small town."

"I can't just pretend I don't know that there's a threat," Curtis objected. "According to the photos he attached to his most recent letter, he knows you're traveling."

"What do you mean he knows I'm traveling?"

"He included pictures of you at the airport in LA. I don't know that he knows *exactly* where you're going, but that doesn't make me worry any less. He's smart, and he knows how to stay in the shadows. That's why we have yet to catch him."

"What do you want me to do?" I asked, already feeling frustrated with the situation.

"Your safety is the biggest concern right now, so let's figure out how to keep you safe." I knew he meant well, but it didn't make me feel any better.

"Alright. I'm staying with my mom, but I don't want to put her in danger. Maybe I should check into a hotel instead?"

"I feel like that would be even riskier. Even with extra locks in place, that doesn't guarantee that he won't find you there. Or worse, that he won't be able to get in. We've already had an issue with him showing up at your house and you have security in place there, remember?"

"Are you fucking serious?" Aiden questioned, his jaw tense again.

"As a heart attack," Curtis responded. "We've been trying to figure out who he is for months but can't catch him. He signs everything as Kevin, but we don't even know if that's really his name. Everything he does is very calculated and planned out."

"I can't stay with my mom," I objected, chewing my lower lip between my teeth. "A hotel is going to have to do because there aren't any other options."

"Yes, there are," Aiden interrupted, his green eyes blazing as they found mine again. "She's staying with me."

"Please don't take this the wrong way, but how can I be sure this is a safe option for her?" Curtis questioned.

"Because I would die before I would let anything happen to her."

Chills ran up my spine as he reached for my hand and squeezed it.

"Sorry for interrupting," Jackie said, stepping closer. "I just wanted to assure you that we take care of our own in Sugarplum Falls. You don't have to worry about Makayla's safety. I'll work on letting everyone in town know to be extra cautious with any outsiders they encounter, and I'll help keep an eye on her. Aiden and I both carry, and I have yet to miss my mark."

"Well, shit. Maybe I should up and move to Sugarplum Falls… Sounds like a safe place to me."

"Thanks for the update, Curtis. I'll keep you posted on whether I need anything."

"Sounds good. I'll note that you'll be staying with Aiden, but when you get a chance, send me his info so I can get in touch if needed. I know you don't want it, but I'm still going to send a few guys out there, just to be safe."

"I don't think that's necessary," I objected, not wanting to tell him that I, in fact, would not be staying with Aiden.

"But it is. Stop trying to plot things behind my back. I know you better than that, Makayla," Curtis warned.

Before I could say anything, Aiden snatched my phone out of my hand and walked off as he rattled off his info for Curtis.

"Guess you have a new roommate," Jackie teased, setting her stuff down on the counter behind the bar.

"So it seems."

"Want me to make you a drink? You seem a bit frazzled."

"Do you have anything strong enough to handle living with Aiden?"

She looked past me to where he was standing in the corner, arms folded over his chest and brows pinched together from whatever it was Curtis was telling him as he held my phone out in front of him.

"Honey, I don't think there's anything in the world that's strong enough to prepare you for living with him. But we can try."

Eleven
Aiden

"This is the guest room, but as you can see, it's not set up for guests," I said with a heavy sigh, ignoring how my body felt having Makayla in such close proximity. The room was packed full of boxes that I had recently moved in while clearing out the garage.

"That's okay. I can sleep on the couch," she said as if she had a choice.

"I don't think so." I placed my hand on her lower back and guided her down the hallway to the master bedroom at the end. "You'll be staying in my room with me."

"No, I won't."

She turned to walk off instead of going into the room. I knew she was stubborn, but this was a new level, even for her.

"Yes, you will." I tried pushing her in as gently as I could, but when she wouldn't stop resisting, I had enough and tossed her over my shoulder before depositing her on the bed.

"Aiden!" she shrieked, eyes wide and mixed with a combination of shock and arousal. "You can't just manhandle me like that."

"I can if you're not going to do what I say."

"And since when are you the boss of me?" She sat in the middle of the bed with her hands planted firmly on her hips.

"Since I found out you have an obsessed stalker, Makayla. How do you think I'm going to protect you if you're in the living room, sleeping on my couch?"

She worried her lower lip between her teeth as she stared at me.

"Well, obviously, they would have to break in, and you would hear that," she answered with a soft shrug.

"Wrong. If this guy is as good as Curtis says, I'm not taking any chances. And you shouldn't either, Makayla. Do you have some sort of death wish or something?"

"No. Why would you say that?"

"Because you're making it awfully hard to protect you when you're fighting me on everything."

She lowered her head and sighed heavily, her chest rising and falling with the motion.

"If I don't fight you, then that means I'm letting my guard down, and I can't do that."

"And why not?" I stepped closer to the bed, needing to be next to her.

"Because if I let my guard down, I'll fall in love again. Neither of us needs that to happen."

I nodded as the air rushed out of me. She looked so beautiful sitting on my bed, almost as if she belonged there.

"Well, I guess it's too late for that because *I* never stopped loving you."

I could hear the blood rushing in my ears as my heart beat wildly in my chest.

Did I just tell Makayla I still loved her?

Her head whipped up and cocked to the side, studying me as if she expected me to tell her it was some sort of joke. But it was anything but that.

"You love me?"

"Always have. Always will." I shoved my hands into my pockets to keep from reaching out to touch her.

"Aiden," she whispered, shaking her head. "You're not supposed to be in love with me."

"Yeah, well, try telling that to my heart."

She looked up at me with a mix of emotions on her face that made my heart flutter.

"Why don't I show you the rest of the house?" I offered, hoping to change the subject before things got even more awkward between us.

She nodded and climbed off the bed, seeming even more unsure about staying with me. I didn't want to make her feel uncomfortable by telling her I loved her. Hell, I didn't even mean to tell her. But I needed her to know that she meant the world to me, and I wasn't lying when I told Curtis that I would die protecting her.

I gave her a quick tour of the house and then got lunch started while she waited for her mom to come by to drop off her stuff. Jackie had taken care of alerting those in town who would be essential in keeping Makayla safe—which meant she told those who could actually do something and not those who would just sit around and gossip about it.

My mind had been a jumbled mess from the moment I saw her the other night, but now it was like everything had been cleared, and there was only one goal I needed to focus on— keeping the woman I loved safe from harm.

Twelve
Makayla

"I don't think it's a good idea for me to go tonight," I said, saying goodbye to my mom at the door.

I didn't want to tell her what was going on with my stalker—especially since I knew she would be disappointed that I'd kept it from her for this long. But deciding in the spur of the moment to stay with Aiden meant I had to come clean and tell her what was really going on. It wasn't that I was excited about staying with him, but it made the most sense. The last thing I needed was for her to get her hopes up that something was going on between us when there wasn't.

If anything, it made me even more tense and stressed because he had confessed he was still in love with me. There was a time when I would have given the world to hear him say those words again, but now that he'd said them, I almost wished he hadn't. Now wasn't the right time for anything to try to happen between us, and I couldn't help but wonder if he would have still said them had he not found out someone was stalking me. If there wasn't the element of my life being in danger, would he still have admitted it—better yet, would he still feel the same?

"Okay, dear. I understand. I can't say that I'm happy about not knowing you've had a stalker this whole time, but it does make me feel better that you're going to stay with

Aiden. I know he'll take good care of you."

Not in the way I would like him to take care of me because that would involve feelings, and no one needed to catch those at a time like this.

I smiled tightly and nodded my head, unable to get words out that wouldn't be sarcastic. At this point, it was better not to say anything at all.

"I'm glad you'll be staying at Brock's house when you can," I said, hating that there would be times when she wouldn't have him there because of his work schedule.

"I'll talk to the ladies and see what they want to do about rehearsing. I think doing it at Sugar Faced Bar during the day is still the best idea, but we'll have to see if that works for Aiden. I don't want to make things any harder for him than they already are. We have less than two weeks until the competition, so we can't mess around."

"Sounds good, mom. Text me once you get home so I know you're okay."

"Why wouldn't I be okay?" she asked, eyebrows immediately raised.

Goosebumps spread quickly across my skin as I realized that my mom has always lived in Sugarplum Falls, and aside from suspense movies, she's never had to experience something like this in real life. I didn't want to scare her by telling her that there was a chance my stalker would show up in town or, even worse—that he would find her and use her to get to me.

"It's just something they say in the big city," Aiden assured her as he came up behind me and rested his hand on my lower back.

I tried to ignore the flames that spread through me from the contact as my mother narrowed her eyes and looked between us to figure out who was lying.

"Yeah," I agreed, my voice shakier than I would have liked. "I'm so used to saying it that it just slipped off my tongue." I rolled my eyes, trying to get her to believe it, but I felt her still judging me.

"Okay…" She stepped outside and cast one more glance at us over her shoulder before heading to her car. Once she was inside and pulling away, Aiden closed the door and locked it.

I leaned against the wall and closed my eyes.

"How am I supposed to do this?" I whined, hating that I had brought this problem to the one place my mother should feel safe.

"We'll figure it out as we go. You don't have to worry about her right now. I have someone watching her."

"You have someone watching my mom?" I asked, tilting my head to look at him.

He nodded.

"Aiden," I said with a heavy sigh. "You don't need to do all of this. I promise it's fine. Curtis already insisted on sending a few guys from my security team out. I'm sure they'll be popping up and struggling to blend in any minute now."

"They're actually set to arrive this evening. Their flight was delayed."

My eyebrows rose high into my hairline as I stared at him.

"You know when my security team is arriving?"

"I do. I know their names, what they look like, and I have a full background check on both of them."

"You're kidding me, right?"

"Not one bit."

He walked off and headed back to the kitchen as I trailed behind him.

"Aiden," I blurted out, my frustration quickly mounting. "How exactly did you get this information?"

"Curtis," he replied, his back to me as he pulled a dish out of the oven. I didn't want to judge because it smelled *amazing,* but who the hell had this kind of time to make such an elaborate meal for lunch? Hadn't he heard of sandwiches?

"So Curtis just handed over information that is supposed to be confidential and classified?" I pressed, moving out of the way as he worked around me to get lunch set up.

"Yes. We talked, and I told him that in order to keep you safe, I needed to have this information. He sent it over a while ago, and I made it a top priority to go over it as soon as I got it."

I closed my eyes and let my head fall back.

"I think everyone is making a bigger deal out of this than it needs to be."

Before I could open my eyes, I felt him stand in front of me, pinching my chin in between his fingers to get my attention.

"This is a big deal, Makayla. If I don't know who he is sending, then this Kevin guy can easily walk in and pretend to be someone on your security team. I refuse to let him get that close to you without knowing everything I can about everyone who shows up in Sugarplum Falls. You might not want to take this seriously, but I do. So does everyone in this town. So suck it up, buttercup. This is happening whether you like it or not."

He stepped back, his green eyes blazing with heat as my body tried to process what just happened. I should have been annoyed by how he was treating me, but at the same time, I found it very arousing. Which was bad given that I was doing my best to make sure that line between us *didn't* get crossed again.

58

Thirteen
Aiden

"Thank you for covering tonight, Jackie. I really appreciate it." I held the phone between my ear and neck as I gathered the papers that were coming out of the printer in my office.

"Not a problem. I'll let you know if anyone out of place shows up, but I think it's going to be a quiet night."

I finished the call and then took the papers to the living room while Makayla soaked in a bath. I knew she needed it, even if she refused. Plus, it gave me time to sit down and go over everything Curtis had sent me.

After fighting with Makayla over lunch about the level of security she needed, I got on the phone with Curtis and asked him to give me everything they had on this Kevin guy. I knew he'd already done a background check on me and Jackie and that he would be doing them on the rest of the people I told him would be watching over Makayla while she was here. The nice thing was that he didn't try to act like a pompous ass, and his focus was the same as mine—keeping her safe.

Her security team had landed half an hour ago and had to drive the rest of the way into Sugarplum Falls, so I expected them to arrive shortly. They were to go directly to the hotel and appear to be regular tourists until we could get a handle on what was going on. He had sent me images of the letters and gifts that had been sent to her, which was what I was now going through.

My jaw tensed as I flipped through the pages, reading the letters and notes from someone clearly obsessed with her. Why they hadn't taken more action on this sooner was beyond me. This guy was clearly a threat to her safety, and the fact he had gotten into her house had my blood boiling.

I heard footsteps and gathered the papers before Makayla walked into the living room.

"What all did he send you?" she asked, pointing at the stack I was trying to hide.

I tried to ignore the soft lavender scent that floated around her as she sat on the couch and tucked her legs beneath her.

I pulled my shoulders back and turned to face her, deciding to be honest with her.

"Everything I asked for. Information on your security team, how long everyone has worked there, what they do. Information on the studio you use, people you've worked with, people you might have had conflict with." I took a deep breath and let it out slowly. "And everything he has on Kevin."

She nodded but didn't appear to be as angry as I imagined she would be.

"He was in my bedroom. My assistant found him sniffing my underwear." She reached forward and grabbed a photo from the floor I hadn't realized had dropped from the stack. "I wasn't home, thank goodness. I was out of state at the time. But I haven't felt comfortable going back ever since. It's like he took something from me by being there. I travel as often as I can and renewed my tour, just so I didn't have to go home."

I shook my head in frustration for her and the shitty situation someone else put her in.

"I'm so sorry."

She shrugged and set the photo on the table before looking at me.

"I try to protect myself the best I can. I constantly pay attention to my surroundings. I don't go anywhere without checking in with Curtis to let him know where I'm going and when I plan to be back. I play by the book, yet this guy thinks the rules don't apply to him. It drives me crazy."

"I can imagine. But what I don't get is why you didn't tell me this was happening?"

"Why would I?"

"Because I can protect you, Makayla," I said, aggravated that she didn't understand how much this bothered me.

"As much as I love that you want to, it's not that easy."

"Why not?"

"Because we live two very different lives, Aiden. You can't just drop everything every time something happens to me. Your life is here, and I love that for you. But my life is very different. I travel a lot and spend the majority of my time on tour when I'm not stuck in the studio for hours recording new albums. Add in press conferences and social obligations, and there's very little time for me to do anything else. That wouldn't be fair to you, and I would never ask you to give up or sacrifice the things that bring you happiness."

"*You* bring me happiness. Knowing that you're safe brings me happiness," I countered, even though I knew it didn't matter.

She inhaled slowly and then released it through pursed lips.

"You deserve more than I could ever give you, Aiden. If you can't see that, that's fine. But I know it, and I won't allow you to sell yourself short, even if it's for me. I appreciate you letting me stay with you while we figure out my next step, but you don't have to do all this extra work to protect me. My security team is in place, so they can take it from here."

She got up and walked away, leaving me alone and frustrated.

Fourteen
Makayla

"Good morning. May I please get a large gingerbread latte?" I asked, trying to ignore the tension radiating off of me as the two guys sent from my security team stood beside me.

They weren't the guys I usually worked with, and when I questioned Curtis about it, he said that he had little to work with on such short notice. Then he proceeded to go on about how some people take vacations this time of year and that I should ignore them the best I could and enjoy my time in town with my mom.

Sam smiled and entered my order into the computer.

"Anything for you guys?" he asked, leaning around me to make eye contact with them.

They didn't answer, just gave a slight shake of their head to say no and resumed their watch of the small space inside of Sugarplum Lattes.

"How are things going?" He grabbed a to-go cup and then started making my drink.

"Fine. I guess." I shrugged, hating that I felt like I couldn't talk or be myself with these goons hanging around. "I would love it if I didn't have to have the security detail, but here we are."

"I can understand that," he replied over his shoulder as he frothed the milk. "But given the circumstances, it's for the best."

"I know," I agreed with a heavy sigh as I took my drink from him. "Thanks for the coffee."

He nodded and attempted to smile at the guys, but it wasn't returned.

"Andi has fudge this morning. You might want to stop in and grab some before you get your day started. It always has a way of turning mine around when I need it."

I smiled and gave him a little wave before heading out, heavy footsteps falling in line behind me.

By the time I entered Sugarplum Sweets, I was ready to scream for people to stop staring at us. It wasn't just that I was back in town and people hadn't seen me in years or that most people recognized me as a celebrity. I could handle all of that. What I couldn't handle was the people talking behind their hands about the guys sent to protect me. While they were supposed to blend in, they did anything but that, looking like they were taken straight out of the *Men In Black* movie. Not that they looked extraterrestrial or anything, but I wouldn't be surprised if they were in fact alien, given how little personality they had.

"Hey, how's it going?" Andi called as soon as she came out and saw me. Her eyes went from happy to see me to confused as she saw the guys behind me.

"Fine. Everything is just fine," I lied, plastering on the best fake smile I could. "Sam said you have fudge."

Andi chuckled and walked behind the counter to the end by

the register, where there was a small basket of fudge.

"I sure do." She handed it to me and then nodded for me to follow her over to one of the small tables in the corner.

I looked inside to decide which piece to take since there were so many to choose from.

"Just bring the whole thing," she said, smiling. "Zach is making more so we can finish what's in there. You two can help yourself to some sugar cookies." She looked directly at the security guys, stopping them in their tracks as she pointed to the other end of the counter with more samples. "She's fine. Seriously. She's with me, and the only way in or out of the store is through those doors."

I laughed as she gave them a pointed look and scolded them like a mother.

Reluctantly, they both made their way to the cookies and then kept their backs against the wall as they continuously surveyed the room.

"They are intense," she whispered, leaning in so only I could hear as I set the basket of fudge down on the table between us.

"You're telling me," I groaned, popping a piece of maple pecan fudge into my mouth and closing my eyes the second the incredible flavor hit my tastebuds.

"How long are they going to be doing *this* for?"

"I have no idea. Hopefully not too long, but I'm guessing until I leave and go back to LA."

She scrunched her face as I popped another piece of fudge into my mouth. I was killing time and needing to distance myself from Aiden this morning. Not that I would be getting too much space from him, given that my mom had made arrangements for us to rehearse at the bar again. I'd convinced Aiden to let me get coffee and breakfast before I met them there, and he only agreed because Sam and a few of the other shop owners in the strip mall were part of *Sugarplum Falls Security Detail*, as he liked to call it.

"I'm sorry. But hey, it's better to be safe than sorry," she said softly with a smile.

"True. I hate that we have to worry about this to begin with."

My phone vibrated in my pocket, so I pulled it out to find a text message from my mom, letting me know that she and the ladies were on their way to the bar.

"I guess I better get going. I'm supposed to meet the Sugarplum Sweethearts to rehearse for the caroling competition. Thanks for the fudge. Sam was right; it did turn my mood around slightly."

"Good," Andi said, standing up and walking with me. "Let me send you with some so it keeps your day going in the right direction."

"Sounds wonderful. Thank you."

I stood at the register and waited for her to finish boxing some up so I could pay.

"It's on the house," she insisted as I tried to hand her my credit card.

"No, really. Let me pay."

She shook her head and extended the box to me.

"You have more than enough on your plate this morning," she commented, nodding to the two guys who were already heading toward me. "It's my treat."

"Well, thank you. I appreciate it."

I turned and almost bumped into one of them as he stood a mere inch away from me. I raised my eyebrows and stared at him until he took a step back.

I shook my head and inhaled deeply as I headed to my car, wondering if I could get in and speed off before they could get in.

Fifteen
Aiden

"Seriously, I got it from here. You guys can watch the perimeter. She's safe inside with me," I said for the fifteenth time to the bodyguards who had been assigned to Makayla.

They were obsessive and I could tell that she wasn't a fan of them the way she rushed in and took Jackie up on her offer to help stock supplies in the back. We didn't have anything that needed to be stocked, but it was a great excuse to get her away from them.

"We won't be far," the older one said, his voice gruff as he pushed his sunglasses back up his nose and turned to leave.

Why they were wearing sunglasses and black suits was beyond me. The whole point of getting someone down here to help with security was to keep her safe, not draw even more attention to her.

I closed the door and pulled my phone out of my pocket to call Curtis. By the second ring, he answered.

"Hey, I don't want to sound like a dick because I'm grateful that you sent a security detail down here for Makayla, but can I ask what in the world you were thinking with sending those two?"

He laughed on the other end, which helped lighten my mood.

"Those guys aren't her real detail. Her regular security team was unavailable, but I pulled a few strings yesterday, AKA I offered a huge holiday bonus, and two of them should be arriving today. I'll send over their information here in a few, along with their travel details. For now, she's going to have to deal with the other two until they've officially been relieved of duty."

"Does she know about the change?"

"Not yet. I've been busting my ass all night and most of the morning to get things settled. I'll send her a text here in a few to let her know."

"Sounds good. Let me know if there's anything you need from me in the meantime. She's at the bar with me today so she can rehearse with the choir for the competition. I haven't figured out things for this evening yet since I'm supposed to work, but I'll make sure she's taken care of."

"Just go about business as usual. Her team is highly trained and knows what to do. Your best bet right now is to continue as if there isn't a threat."

"Easier said than done," I said, shoving a hand through my hair.

"I know. But right now, that's the best we can do. I'll have my cell phone on if you guys need anything."

"Thanks, Curtis."

I hung up the phone and rolled my head on my neck as I tried to alleviate some of the mounting tension.

"Are they gone?" Makayla asked, coming back into the bar with Jackie behind her.

"They're securing the perimeter outside. I told them to keep watch out there and that we have things covered in here."

"Thank you. I appreciate that."

"No problem." I smiled as I glanced at the boxes Jackie had brought out this morning. "But since you're here and the Sugarplum Sweethearts aren't here to rehearse, I'm putting you to work."

"Work?" she asked with a soft laugh. "I don't want to brag or anything, but I can make a killer rum and Coke. Also, why am I not surprised they're not here yet? I swear, my mom is the worst with being on time lately."

"Not that kind of work."

I folded my arms over my chest and enjoyed watching her squirm.

"Do you want me to clean?" She glanced around the room, relief on her face that it was already clean.

"Nope. You're going to help us decorate."

"Decorate?"

"For Christmas."

Her brows pulled together as I walked over to the first box and opened it up. Inside were a handful of decorations that we put up every year. I pulled out the giant piece of artificial mistletoe and held it up.

"It's still like three weeks until Christmas. Isn't it a bit early?"

I heard Jackie gasp behind me and chuckled.

"Not in Sugarplum Falls. We're technically a little behind on decorating, and since I don't want to be the center of the town's gossip, I figured we'd better get them up today."

Makayla shook her head and grinned.

"I totally forgot how Christmas-obsessed this town is."

"Do you not decorate this early in LA?" Jackie asked, grabbing another box and setting it on the floor.

"I, um, I don't usually decorate." Makayla scrunched her face as the words came out, this time earning her a gasp from both of us.

"You don't decorate for Christmas?" I questioned, my head cocked to the side as I stared in disbelief.

"I don't usually have time. Things are always so busy, and by the time I get home, it's days before Christmas, and it just feels pointless to decorate when I'm the only one who would see it."

"Do you spend the day by yourself too?" I pressed, not loving this at all.

She shrugged and looked away before answering.

"Sometimes. But my mom and I always FaceTime. So it's not like I'm *alone* alone."

"Makayla, Makayla, Makayla," I said with a sigh.

"What?" She laughed, her eyes wide as she watched Jackie and me.

"That's a big problem, but don't worry. We know how to solve it." I looked from her to Jackie, who nodded.

"Fix what?"

"I'll call for reinforcements," Jackie said, pulling her phone out of her pocket and making a call.

"Good call. I'll reach out to Andi for help as well. Don't worry, Makayla, we got you."

"Got me for what? What's going on?" I could hear the confusion in her voice but loved the way her face lit up with wonder.

"We're going to remind you how we do Christmas in Sugarplum Falls."

74

Sixteen
Makayla

"Are you kidding me?" I laughed harder, tossing my head back at how crazy all of this was.

"We don't joke when it comes to Christmas," Sam said, breezing past me with two trays filled with to-go cups of coffee while a kid wearing a Sugarplum Lattes shirt followed behind him with two more.

"I can't believe this." I shook my head, staring in disbelief as the quiet bar was now filled with people from all over town who had joined together to help us decorate. Not only that, they brought a whole freaking party with them.

Andi showed up with containers filled with sugar cookies and stuff to decorate them. Sam brought our caffeine fix. A sweet girl named Hadley came from Sugarplum Gifts with new decorations Aiden had ordered sometime during the madness of everything. There were a few other people who all came to help out which made my heart feel all warm and fuzzy.

"I wasn't sure if you were ready to mix up your drink options yet," Sam said, holding a cup in each hand. "So, I brought a gingerbread latte as well as a salted caramel latte, just in case you were getting tired of the gingerbread one."

"I don't think I could ever get tired of it," I said with a laugh before reaching for the other one. "But I'm learning that change can be good, so I'll give this one a try. Thank you."

"You're welcome."

"No candy canes today?" Aiden questioned as he walked past us to the bar and looked at the cups lining it with names written on them. Once he found his, he lifted it to his lips and frowned before taking a drink.

"I brought you your usual, you big baby," Sam said, watching as Aiden's features changed once he took a drink.

"What's your usual?" I asked, curious what kind of coffee he drank these days.

"Nothing special. Just plain black coffee."

"He plays it off like it's just plain black coffee, but technically, he's been getting a black eye, which adds two shots of espresso to it. It's like he's not sleeping well or something," Sam said with enough sarcasm that everyone in the room picked up on it.

"It's that sweet coffee crap you sent over that's had me up all night," Aiden countered, lifting his cup to take another drink.

"I've been meaning to ask, what's the deal with the candy canes?" I asked Sam, curious to hear his explanation.

His cheeks flushed an adorable shade of red before he answered.

"My grandpa used to tell me that the key to solving a lover's quarrel was to sit down, have a cup of coffee, and eat candy canes. By themselves, they're just candy canes, but put them together, and they make a heart. It's obvious that you and Aiden have had a lover's quarrel, so I just thought candy canes were fitting." He shrugged, but I barely noticed it as I caught Aiden's eye.

"Alright, everyone, are we ready to get the sugar cookie decorating started?" Andi called out, interrupting the moment, which was probably for the best.

Sam smiled and walked off to join the others as Aiden placed his hand on my lower back and guided me over. It was the new thing he did, and I didn't mind it at all. It was comforting and made me feel safe and protected, even if my body craved his touch elsewhere.

"Today we're going to get our hands dirty and make some fun by—"

"This isn't the toddler decorating class," a cute guy off to the side said, making Andi pause.

"Oh my gosh," she said with a laugh. "I swear, I do that class so often that the words just roll out of my mouth without thinking about it. Sorry, guys. Anyway, we're going to welcome Makayla home by showing her how we do Christmas in Sugarplum Falls. Things are a lot different here than in the big city. We've brought plenty of cookies to decorate, but if you need anything, just holler. Zach or I will make our way around to check how everyone is doing."

"You know you didn't have to do all of this, right?" I asked Aiden as he led me to one of the tables and pulled a chair out for me.

"I know I don't *have* to do anything. I wanted to."

Andi set a plate of sugar cookies down on our table before rushing off to grab the stuff to decorate them with. The door opened and I expected to see the guys from my security team, but was surprised to see my mom and the ladies from the choir instead.

I got up and walked over to help take some of the bags my mom was struggling to carry.

"What is all of this?" I asked, noticing the crockpots that were being lined up on the bar where the coffee cups had been.

"Lunch." My mom smiled and then started unloading the stuff from the bags.

"What?"

"We brought lunch. Aiden called and told me what was happening, so I rallied the ladies, and we all put together lunch for everyone since we were heading over to rehearse anyway. It made me a few minutes late, but I don't mind. I brought pulled pork and stuff to make sandwiches. Shirley made her famous chili, and Susie brought a peach cobbler for dessert. Linda is on her way, and she's bringing beef stew."

"Aiden called you too?" I asked, not wanting to poke the bear by reminding her that she was more than just *a few minutes* late.

"He did. He also told me that you haven't been decorating for Christmas," she lowered her voice as she looked around, making sure no one else could hear.

"Sorry, mom. I've been a little busy."

"Well, we should still make time for the important stuff. The nice thing is that you're spending Christmas in Sugarplum Falls this year, so we're going to make sure it's the best Christmas ever. You better get over there and start decorating your cookies. We're a highly competitive bunch, and I don't want to brag, but I decorate the best cookies. I would hate to take out my own daughter, but I will."

"Okay, okay," I said with a laugh, holding my hands in front of me. "I don't know what you've done with my mom, but I like this."

She swatted my butt playfully as I made my way back to the table Aiden was sitting at, admiring how cute he looked as he worked on decorating his cookie.

BLAME IT ON THE CAROLS

Seventeen
Aiden

"I can't let you be the winner, given what you did to Rudolph," Andi said, her hands planted firmly on her hips.

"What? He's just catching a ride." I shrugged and smiled at the two reindeer-shaped sugar cookies I had cleverly attached together to make it look like one was riding the other. I'd also gone to the extreme by taking a piece of a broken antler and using it to make it look like one had an erection. What could I say? It was fun and there weren't any kids around. Plus, I liked the way Makayla blushed when she saw it.

"You're as bad as Sam." She shook her head and walked off.

"What did he make?" I asked, genuinely intrigued. I got up and went to his table, where I found everyone else gathered.

Sam had taken one of the full-length Santa cookies and very intricately painted it to look like Santa's pants were down. He then strategically placed one of the small round ornament-shaped cookies on top of it and painted it to be Mrs. Claus giving Santa a treat of her own.

"How did you get that to line up so well?" I asked, pointing to Mrs. Claus.

"I used a knife and very carefully cut the back of the cookie until it was super thin. Then I attached it with a thin layer of frosting and painted her head onto it," he explained.

"I'm telling you, Andi, there's a whole market you're missing with adult-only cookie decorating classes," Jasmin said, nodding her head as she admired Sam's work. Jasmin ran the town's Frosty Fest and stopped by to help get things decorated for us before the bar opened tonight.

It wasn't like it was a big deal if it wasn't decorated before we opened. It was more important to me that Makayla had fun and saw what the town was really about. Not only that, we could literally decorate while the bar was open and more than half of our patrons would jump in to help. That's just what happens in small towns.

"You guys are making it hard to pick a winner," Andi groaned, holding her hands over her face when she realized what she'd said. "Difficult. You guys are making it *difficult*. I can't pick. Zach, you're going to have to choose a winner."

"You can't let him pick," Jackie objected. "He's going to pick one of the perverted ones these two knuckleheads did. You need someone who will see the true artistic abilities and care taken when decorating the perfect sugar cookie." She held hers up like Vanna White for everyone to see.

"No way," Jill said, standing up and holding her cookie in the air. "No one is going to beat me this year. I present to you the winning sugar cookie."

"It's just a stocking," Sam objected, ducking as she walked past and swatted at his head.

"It is *not* just a stocking. It's a beautiful red velvet stocking with white fur trim and glitter. It's perfect."

"I can't pick," Andi said again, lifting her arms helplessly in the air.

I went back to the table and glanced down at Makayla's cookie she had been working on. I had been so caught up in creating a naughty one that I hadn't noticed what she had done.

"We have the winner right here," I said, still staring down at it.

Andi made her way over, followed by everyone else. There were soft gasps as they stared at the perfection I couldn't take my eyes off of.

In front of Makayla sat three tree-shaped cookies with white royal icing to make it look like snow. She then added green frosting, making the perfect ridges to look like branches, and then brown at the bottom for the trunk. Each branch had white icing that was piped on to look like snow, while some had specks of glitter to make it look like it was freshly fallen.

"They're just trees," she said softly, shrugging as her cheeks flushed with embarrassment from everyone watching.

"They're not just trees," Andi replied before I could. "Makayla, the level of detail you have on these blow my mind. This is amazing. If you're ever looking for a job in town, I would hire you in a heartbeat to make cookies like this for me."

My heart jumped at her words, wishing it was something Makayla would consider even though I knew better.

"Thank you. I appreciate that."

"We have our winner," Andi announced. "Here's your prize."

She pulled a small envelope out of her back pocket and gave it to Makayla.

"It's a fifty-dollar gift card to Sugarplum Sweets. Congratulations, you knocked it out of the park with those."

Andi smiled and walked off while Makayla held the envelope in her hands, staring in disbelief.

"I can't believe I won."

"I can. Those are amazing. You're very talented."

"It was actually quite therapeutic," she replied with a laugh. "It let me get out of my head for a while, and before I knew it, I was on a roll."

"I'm glad it helped."

"All of this has, Aiden. You went out of your way to bring all of these wonderful people together just to show me what Christmas can be like and it's not even Christmas yet. No one has ever done something like this for me before. Christmases with my mom in Sugarplum Falls were always great, but I've never seen an entire town come together like that. We always just stayed home and celebrated together. We didn't have a lot of money, so she worked a lot, which meant we didn't do stuff like decorate cookies or spend a lot of time with people."

"You deserve it, Mak. You deserve all the joy and happiness in the world, and if I can help give it to you, I will."

"I'm so lucky to have a friend like you," she said softly, looking away before she could see the hurt in my eyes.

85

BLAME IT ON THE CAROLS

Eighteen
Makayla

It had been over a week since Aiden arranged the little holiday party for me at the bar. I hadn't been able to stop thinking about how wonderful it felt to have everyone drop what they were doing to join us. I had forgotten what small-town life felt like after being in the city and constantly in a rush for so long. My mom had come to LA to visit a handful of times when I couldn't make it home, but it wasn't the same. Having my mom around was wonderful, but there was something to be said about what this town could do to someone. It was almost like it filled an emptiness in my heart that had been hollow for so long. Or perhaps that was from being around Aiden so much.

I also hadn't been able to get the sad look on his face out of my mind after telling him that he was such a great friend. But what was I supposed to say? We both knew that the love we once shared was still there, but I wasn't stupid enough to think that things would work any differently for us now than they had six years ago when I left.

I sat on the couch, going through the brochure my mother had given me for the competition tomorrow. I had expected it to be on some grander scale with lots of other choirs they were competing against, but it turned out there were only five total, including the Sugarplum Sweethearts. I would have laughed at how ridiculous my mother had been when she obsessed over how they *had to win this*, but being back in Sugarplum Falls made me remember just how competitive everyone was. From decorating houses to sugar cookie decorating, there was a competition for everything.

It felt weird being in the house without Aiden, but I was thankful that he had at least relaxed a little bit and allowed me some space once my real security detail arrived. I was more than happy to say farewell to the Men In Black and sighed a breath of relief when greeted by Tony and Patrick once they got to town. They were so good at what they did that I didn't even feel or notice their presence most of the time.

My phone vibrated on the table, the noise startling me.

"Hello," I answered, pressing it to my ear without bothering to check the caller ID.

"Hi, Makayla," a deep voice answered, sending chills immediately down my spine. I jolted up and scanned the room for Tony or Patrick, not even a few seconds passed by before Tony was by my side. His brows furrowed in concern as I nodded my head.

"Hi, Kevin." My voice was shaky but not as shaky as my fingers that trembled trying to hold the phone. "How did you get my phone number?"

Tony motioned for me to keep him talking while Patrick held his phone to his ear, pacing behind us.

"Don't you know, I know everything about you, Makayla. Those sugar cookies you decorated were quite amazing, weren't they?"

My eyes widened as I tried to fight back the tears. Aiden

chose that moment to come home and walked in with a smile on his face that was immediately replaced with concern. He rushed over but stayed quiet after Tony pressed his finger to his lips. I pulled the phone away from my ear for a moment and put the call on speakerphone so they could hear it.

"Thank you. I didn't know you had seen the sugar cookies that I decorated."

I could feel the tension around me as Tony quickly swiped his fingers across his phone and then held it up to show us an image of the front page of the Sugarplum Gazette. Right there in the middle of the screen was a picture of the cookies I'd decorated with a caption that read: *Local music superstar Makayla Rhodes wins sugar cookie decorating contest with gorgeous hand-painted snow-covered pine trees.*

"I see everything. I'll admit, I'm glad you got rid of those goons they originally sent you. They were so obvious."

I shrugged my shoulders, unsure of how to answer that. He was clearly in town and watching me without any of us knowing where he was. Aiden went through the house quickly closing the blinds and checking to make sure the doors were locked.

"Yeah, they were the worst," I said, just throwing words out there to keep him talking while Patrick continued his conversation.

"It's so silly that they sent security for you anyway."

"Why is that?"

"Because you don't need it. You have me."

I tried to breathe slowly to keep the nausea at bay as bile rose in my stomach.

"I would never hurt you, Makayla. You know that. I buy you stuff and send you letters so you know how much I love you. If anything, *I* should be protecting you from *them.*"

Tony and I exchanged a look but it was apparent he didn't know what to say to that either. I looked at Aiden, but he was frowning. His arms were crossed so tightly over his chest that I worried the seams on his t-shirt would burst open.

"I'm so lucky to have so many people who love me," I said softly, wanting him to trust me. "Thank you for the gifts, by the way. I haven't had a chance to say that since things have been so busy."

"You're welcome. Did you find the new lingerie I put in your drawer before you left? I tried to make sure you had everything you needed, but it was more difficult to get into your house than before. If you want to give me the code or a key, that would make things so much easier."

I turned my head and tried to keep control of myself.

"I'm sorry, I don't think I saw them. But I'll definitely have something to look forward to when I return." My jaw hurt from how tightly I was gritting my teeth, trying to force the words out. "I'm assuming you'll be there when I get back?"

"Of course I will. You better go rehearse before the competition tomorrow. You wouldn't want to be the reason the Sugarplum Sweethearts lose this year, would you?"

I opened my mouth but no words came out as the line went dead. Tears filled my eyes as I looked helplessly around the room.

"Who the fuck is this guy?" Aiden growled, looking from Tony to Patrick.

I covered my face in my hands, not wanting them to see me cry as the cushion beside me shifted with Aiden's weight as he sat down and wrapped his arms around me.

"We were able to trace the call this time," Patrick said.

"Where did it come from?" Tony asked.

"He's here. In Sugarplum Falls. Exact location is the mall."

Nineteen
Aiden

"You can't keep missing work because of me," Makayla objected as I checked the doors one last time to make sure everything was locked up and secure.

Curtis had sent over extra security, and I'd talked to Jackie to let her know I wasn't going to be there tonight. She touched base with those in town who were aware of what was going on and asked them to be extra vigilant. Kevin was in town, which meant he should be easy to spot—more or less. Unfortunately, there was always a lot of traffic from neighboring towns, especially the closer we got to Christmas.

"It's fine. Your safety is the only thing that matters right now."

I felt a little better after Tony insisted on having my house swept to make sure there were no cameras or tracking devices inside. Thankfully, everything was clean, and they were pretty confident that Kevin didn't know where Makayla was right now. He obviously knew she was in Sugarplum Falls, but he wasn't lurking outside of my house or the bar looking for her. We now had security monitoring both, just to be sure, as well as a team assigned to her mom. No one was taking any chances with this guy.

Tony was currently sitting outside, watching the house, while Patrick went to the mall to locate Kevin. More security detail had been sent in, but I didn't bother trying to keep up with who was who at this point. Tony and Patrick were our main points of contact, and that was all we needed to know.

"I hate that this is even happening," she said with a sigh. "I should be with my mom and the choir while they rehearse for tomorrow. Instead, I'm stuck hiding out at your house while they try to find this creep."

I arched an eyebrow as I walked past the couch, stopping right in front of her.

"And being stuck at my place is such a bad thing?"

"You know what I mean." She swatted my arm as a smile graced her lips for a split second.

I could see the worry on her face as I came around and sat next to her.

"It's going to be okay, Mak. I promise. They will catch this bastard."

She nodded, her lower lip trembled as she looked away.

I reached over and grabbed her, pulling her into my arms as she quickly fell apart. She cried against my chest, her body shaking as she finally let go. I rubbed my hand soothingly across her back until I felt her start to relax in my embrace.

"I'm so sorry," she said, tilting her head up to look at me. "I shouldn't have come here. I brought this mess with me and put everyone I love in danger."

"Shhh," I whispered, continuing to rub her back. "You didn't put anyone in danger, Mak. It's fine. We have people watching all over town to make sure this prick doesn't do anything stupid."

"I did," she objected, pushing away from me just enough to force me to stop touching her. "My mom. The ladies in the choir. Anyone in this town who gets in his way. You."

"You don't have to worry about that. We're all fine. And you definitely don't have to worry about me. I'm more than—"

I stopped the moment her words hit my brain. Did she just confess she loved me?

I tilted my head and looked at her, watching the crimson wash over her face as she realized I just figured out what she hadn't meant to say.

"Are you saying you love me, Makayla?"

She rubbed her lips and looked up at the ceiling as she pulled a slow, deep breath in.

"Yes. As much as I've tried not to, I can't help it." She wiped the tears from her cheeks with the back of her hand.

"You love me?" I felt stupid for questioning it again, but I needed to hear her say it.

"Yes, you big goof. I love you. There. Are you happy?"

"You have no idea how happy," I replied with a smile that spanned across my face. I reached forward and grabbed her, pulling against my chest again, but this time making sure she couldn't get away.

"That still doesn't change anything, Aiden. If anything, it just makes things harder."

I groaned when she shifted beside me, her breast rubbing against my chest.

"Things are getting hard, that's for sure."

"I know. And this isn't even the hardest it's going to get." She threw her hands in the air, completely oblivious to the situation happening just inches away from her in my pants. "It's going to get so hard that we won't be able to stand it. Then, out of nowhere—boom! It'll all explode in our faces."

I let my head fall back as a chuckle snuck out.

"What are you laughing at?" she whined, smacking me in the chest. "I'm being serious, Aiden. You don't know how hard this is going to get."

"I think I have an idea," I replied, grabbing her hand and lowering it to my crotch.

Her eyes widened as her head whipped up to look at me.

"Aiden!" She laughed but didn't bother removing her hand as I leaned back against the couch and locked my hands behind my head.

"What? I can't help it. You rubbed your boob against my chest, and he got a mind of his own. Then you just kept going on about how hard things were going to get, and he took it as an invitation to demonstrate. However, I am fully on board with things exploding in our faces. I think we should definitely make that happen."

"You're the worst," she teased, gently rubbing me through the thick fabric of my jeans.

"I'm actually the best if you remember correctly."

She looked up and arched an eyebrow at me before leaning into my chest and continuing her torture on my cock that begged to be free.

"What was the record? Four or five orgasms for you in one night?"

"Six." Her cheeks blushed the cutest shade of red as she looked away and focused on my cock. "There was that one that was right on the edge of the other, so it was like one super long, really intense orgasm."

"That's right." I nodded my head, very clearly remembering that night. "That was when you first learned you could squirt."

"And then you didn't let me stop. It became your obsession to see how many times you could make it happen."

"I think I reached pro status."

"I don't think there's such a thing."

"Well, then, I think we should make it a thing. We can start tonight. The first three rounds will be practice until we get back in the groove of things."

"First *three rounds*?"

I nodded again.

"At a minimum."

"How many do you expect there will be?"

I glanced at my watch, checking the time.

"The night is still young. I'd say ten, at minimum."

"I'm going to need another cup of coffee," she joked.

"I can call Sam and request two black eyes if you'd like."

"You're serious about this, aren't you?"

"I don't joke about sex with you, Mak."

"I thought it was *Christmas* people in this town didn't joke about?"

"That's everyone else. For me, I don't joke about being balls deep inside of you as I fuck you senseless. I also don't joke about beating my record of how many times I can make you come in one night."

She licked her lips and then chewed the bottom one nervously.

"Why do I feel like I need to stretch or something before we get started?"

"Because your body remembers what I can do to it. Don't worry, I'll be sure to stretch you real good as I eat your pussy in bed."

I hopped off the couch and grabbed her hand, pulling her with me. When she didn't move as fast as I wanted, I turned around and tossed her over my shoulder, carrying her fireman style to the bed. Fun times were to be had, which meant we didn't have time to waste.

Twenty
Makayla

Aiden tossed me onto his bed like I was some sort of plaything, and I was not upset about it at all. The hunger in his eyes had my pussy aching. Even though I knew we shouldn't be crossing this line, it also felt like now was as good of a time as any.

"I can't tell you how long I've been waiting to eat your pussy again," he admitted as he pulled his shirt over his head and tossed it to the floor, licking his lips.

A chill spread over my body, making me desperate for his touch.

He undressed at record speed, climbing on the bed and quickly removing my clothes. It was as if we both knew how badly we needed this. To touch each other and have the comfort of something familiar. Aiden knew my body better than I did, and I hoped that I still knew all the things that would drive him crazy.

His body was heavy on top of mine, making me needy with desire. I spread my legs, inviting him in as his fingers trailed lightly over my thighs before brushing across my slit. He kissed down the side of my neck, over my collarbone, and then over my breasts. My nipples puckered against the chilly air, hardening more when he drew one into his mouth and sucked.

"Ahh," I cried, scratching my nails down his back as he sucked harder. "Aiden, please."

His chuckle vibrated against my skin as he moved to the other nipple. He slid a finger inside me, the sensation forcing me to squirm on the bed.

"Such a needy little thing, isn't she," he teased as he inserted another finger.

I closed my eyes and arched my back as he continued sucking my nipples with just enough pressure to make it slightly painful but incredibly pleasurable. His thumb brushed over my clit, sending another shockwave through my core as I pressed my thighs together.

"Uh, nope. You're going to give me every single orgasm that I ask for, Mak. No pulling away now," he warned, lowering himself down my body until his face was lined up against my pussy. "Got it?"

I shook my head, feeling too dazed to speak.

"I want to hear you."

"Yes, I got it," I practically cried, my body already overstimulated.

"That's my girl."

Strong hands parted my thighs as I felt the prickle of his stubble scratch my skin. I spread them further, allowing him the access he demanded.

The warmth of his tongue as it swiped across my pussy was almost my undoing. I reached down and gripped his hair, needing something to hold onto as he fucked me with his fingers and sucked my clit.

"Shit," I cried, already feeling the tingle that came right before an orgasm. "I'm so close."

Instinctively, I tried to close my thighs as my legs started to tremble. But Aiden forced them open, holding them in place with his hands as his tongue magically brought me to climax in seconds.

I was gasping and panting by the time he came up, wearing a smirk on his gorgeous face as he wiped his mouth with his hand.

"That wasn't the best you could do, but that's okay. I told you we had some practice runs to get through before we got to the real thing."

"I don't know that my body can handle the real thing. *That* felt pretty real to me."

"Trust me, it can and it will."

I looked down at his cock that was jutting up to his stomach, a drop of precum on the tip. I licked my lips and then sat up, ready to suck him dry.

"As much as I want to come down your throat and watch you gag as you suck my dick, I need to be inside of your pussy first," he said, cupping his hand softly around my chin. "Get on your hands and knees so I can fuck you the way you like."

"How do you know I haven't changed? Maybe I like something else better now instead?" I teased, looking at him over my shoulder.

"Nope. We are not talking about you having sex with anyone else," he whispered in my ear as he slapped my ass playfully, sending another jolt through me.

"I think we both know that was a possibility for *both* of us. We were apart for six years, Aiden."

"Yeah, and now we're together again. I don't care who might've touched this pussy before; no one will ever touch it again. I mean that, Mak. This pussy is mine."

He lined himself up at my opening and waited.

"Did you hear me?"

I nodded, holding my breath as I waited for him to slam into me the way he knew I loved.

"Say it, Mak. I can wait all damn day if I have to. I'm not going to fuck you until you tell me that you know this pussy is mine."

"It's yours," I panted, pushing back against him to try to force his cock inside of me.

"What is?"

His voice was strained, and I knew he was gritting his teeth, trying to stay in control right now.

"This pussy is yours, Aiden. Always has been, always will be."

"Fuck right it is," he agreed, pushing himself inside as I took a shuddered breath.

He felt so much bigger than before, and for a moment, I'd forgotten just how big he was. He gripped my hips with both hands and held me in place while we both took a few seconds to adjust.

"We forgot a condom," I whispered, not interested in having him pull out now. "I've been tested recently and am on the pill."

"I got tested a few months ago when I got my physical done. Do you want me to get one?"

I shook my head, closing my eyes as I pushed back on him and clenched my pussy as tight as I could around his cock.

"I want to feel you without one," I said, slowly grinding against him. "We never did it this way."

"That's because I was trying hard not to get you pregnant back then."

"And now?"

"Now I would love to knock you up and have you carry my child. Just the thought of you pregnant with my baby makes my dick hard."

He reached a hand forward and began rubbing my clit while he fucked me from behind. Feeling him without anything between us was a whole new level of intimacy that I had never felt with anyone before, but with Aiden, it felt right.

The thought of him getting me pregnant turned me on in more ways than I could have imagined, and for just a moment, I allowed myself to envision that fantasy as he brought me to climax shortly before chasing his own.

104

Twenty-One
Aiden

Seven.

That was how many times I made Makayla come before we both had to tap out for the night. When I woke up the next morning to her lying in my arms, hair draped across the pillow, I knew my life would never be the same again. I'd lost her once. I wasn't about to allow it to happen again.

She rolled over, smiling as her eyes fluttered open.

"Good morning," I said, leaning in to kiss her lips.

"Great morning," she replied with a giggle, wrapping her arms around my neck as she tried to pull me down on top of her.

"As much as I would love to devour you this morning, we need to get up so you can get ready."

"My mom's always late. I can be, too."

"Your mom is late to laid-back rehearsals at a bar, Mak. You can't be late to the caroling competition. They would kill you, and then your mom would come after me for allowing you to miss it."

"Ugh. You have a point," she groaned, allowing me to lead her out of bed by the hand.

"Let's take a quick shower, then I'll make you breakfast while you get ready."

"Will you make french toast?"

"I will. And if you're a good girl, I'll even add extra powdered sugar." I booped her nose with my finger, loving the way her eyes lit up with her smile.

I turned the shower on, allowing the water to warm up while she got undressed. It felt weird how easily we'd fallen back into a couple's routine after only being together one night. But she seemed to feel comfortable in my house, helping herself to the things she needed as she paraded around naked like she owned the place.

She stepped into the shower, looking over her shoulder at me as she waited for me to join. My eyes wandered down the curves in her back to the plump ass that begged to be spanked.

"We don't have time for that," she warned, pointing to my growing erection. "Get it under control, Aiden, 'cause there ain't no way in hell that I'm explaining to my mom and the Sugarplum Sweethearts that I'm late due to you having a boner."

I chuckled and headed for her as she closed her eyes and leaned in to let the water run down her face so I could get in behind her.

By the time we finished showering, the water was cold, which was exactly what I needed to get my dick under control. Makayla was here for at least another week—if not longer, which meant I would soak up every second I could with her.

I went to the kitchen to start breakfast while Makayla did her hair and makeup. I tried to ignore the pain I felt in my chest every time I thought about things between us and how nothing was certain. I wanted to talk with her and figure out what all of this meant for us, but now wasn't the time. She needed to focus on the competition, and I wasn't going to stand in the way of that.

"It smells delicious in here," she said, coming into the kitchen with her hair in curlers and makeup done.

"Thank you. Perfect timing, too, because breakfast is ready."

I grabbed her plate and set it on the table before getting the bottle of orange juice out of the fridge. She was already tearing into her French toast before I sat down to join her, which made me happy that she enjoyed my cooking so much.

"Are you ready for today?" I asked, cutting a piece of my french toast with my fork before lifting it to my mouth.

"I think so. I'm pretty nervous, though."

"Why are you nervous? You perform in front of thousands of people all the time. This is on a much smaller scale."

"I know, but there's more on the line with this. When I'm performing on my own, it's because fans have paid money to see me perform. If I screw up, I'm the only one I'm hurting. This is a whole different situation where I'm singing with a choir, and if I don't impress the judges, I'm letting down *hundreds* of people who were counting on me."

"Hundreds?" I questioned with eyebrows raised.

"Yes," she said with a laugh. "Hundreds. Because it's not just the sweet ladies of the Sugarplum Sweethearts that I'm letting down. It's the church they're a part of as much as it is the people of Sugarplum Falls. There's a lot riding on this and I don't want to be the one to mess it up. Trust me, it would be so much easier if my mom would just let me pay for the new roof for them."

"You're not going to let anyone down. I promise. I've heard you sing when you rehearsed with them and you did amazing. You've got this, Mak."

She sighed heavily, her shoulders falling and allowing the thin strap of her bra to slide down. I didn't mind that she came to breakfast wearing her underwear because I was always a sucker for seeing Makayla in lingerie. But this was just pure torture, knowing I couldn't take her to the bedroom and fuck her the way I wanted to.

"Thank you. I really hope so. I know how much they're counting on this win so they can use that money to fix the church's roof."

"It's not just about the money, you do know that, right?"

"Of course I do. It's also about the teamwork and coming together to do something fun."

I shook my head, wiping my face with a napkin as I tried to hide my grin.

"What?" She dropped her fork to her plate and tilted her head to stare at me. "What aren't you telling me?"

"The winner also gets to be in the Frosty Fest parade. There's a whole float, and the winning choir sings carols and tosses candy into the crowd."

"My mom didn't tell me about that. Come to think of it, she didn't mention where the other choirs were from. What if they're not from Sugarplum Falls? Do you guys still allow them to be in the parade?"

"All of the choirs are from here. It's a local competition. There's the Sugarplum Sweethearts, which is the choir you're joining. Then there are the Sugarplum Saints, which is another church in town. We also have the Sugarplum High Choir, which consists of kids from the high school. There's the Sugarplum Singers, which is another school choir but with elementary school students. And, last but not least, there are the Sugarplum Silvers, which is an all-male group over sixty, hence the silver part."

"Oh my gosh!" she shrieked and covered her face. "I cannot go up against *kids*! What if I make them cry because they don't win?"

"It's happened a time or two," I admitted, shrugging. "But you came to do a job, so that's what you need to do. The kids will be fine if they don't win. They'll go to the parade tomorrow morning, get all hyped up on candy canes, and drive their parents crazy as they chase them around the mall. They won't even remember that they lost."

Makayla's eyes widened in horror.

"What have I gotten myself into?"

Twenty-Two
Makayla

It still felt weird to me that there was a caroling competition on a Friday, but now that I knew it was all choirs in Sugarplum Falls, it didn't surprise me. I'd been reminded that things worked differently in a small town than they did in a big city like LA. People moved at their own pace, and if the town said to shut things down because something was happening, that was exactly what everyone did.

I stood in front of the full-length mirror in the breakroom at the mall where the competition was taking place. I had been here a few times when I was younger, but they had changed so much and expanded on it over the past few years, making it much larger than I remembered.

I smoothed a hand over the shimmery red glitter dress I was wearing and caught a glimpse of someone behind me.

"You look amazing," Aiden said, wrapping his arms around my waist and planting a kiss behind my ear.

"Thank you. It feels nice to be dressed up again. I haven't worn something like this in a while."

"Well, stay for New Year's, and we'll get dressed up and go out to celebrate."

I turned to face him, cupping his jaw in my hand.

"I would love that."

He leaned in and kissed the tip of my nose, not wanting to smear the red lipstick I'd just applied.

"You're going to kill it out there," he said, stepping away and letting his eyes rake over my body one more time. "The other choirs have been great, but you're going to blow everyone away."

I inhaled slowly and released it, hoping what he said was true. He waved and left just as my mother walked in.

"You look beautiful, honey," she said, pulling me in for a quick hug. "The ladies are all ready so we thought we'd see if you were so we can get a group picture before we go on stage."

"Of course. Show me the way."

My mother was wearing a gold shimmery dress, much like the one I had on, but with short sleeves and a belt around the waist that had little bells on it. I felt a little self-conscious in the tight dress I had on, especially with the slit up the thigh, but the ladies of the choir had assured me it was perfect. I had no idea what to expect from any of the other choirs, especially since two of them were school-aged children.

"Alright, if you want to stand there in the center, we'll all line up around you," my mother said, pointing to a spot in the middle where the other ladies were standing.

I nodded and got into place, smiling when their bells started clinking from the matching belts they had on.

We got a few photos and then lined up to the side of

the stage where the Sugarplum Silvers were currently performing. I looked back at the ladies behind me, laughing when I noticed how they were all super into the performance. The men all wore matching suits with red blazers and a red and white polka dot tie. Their hair—all silver—was slicked back and their moves were in sync, making me believe they had what it took if they ever wanted to start an elderly boy band. I was honestly surprised by some of their moves, given their age, but I was even more surprised by the way the ladies were hootin' and hollerin' beside me, with the exception of my mom. She already had her silver fox, who just happened to be in the crowd waiting to watch her perform.

"Alright, let's give it up for the Sugarplum Silvers," an older man announced as the men took a quick bow and exited the stage. I felt butterflies in my stomach as he announced us next and the ladies took the lead going up on stage. I was to go on last and take my spot in front.

I gripped the microphone in my hand tighter and carefully made my way up the few stairs to the stage. It was surprising how many people were there in the crowd to watch, but my attention immediately went to the back, where Aiden and Sam were standing. Aiden winked at me, causing the butterflies to swarm wildly in my stomach as I took my place on the X toward the front of the stage.

I lowered my head and focused on my breathing while I waited for the music to start. I had done this what felt like a thousand times, yet I had never performed like this in front of Aiden before.

The music began and the impulse to run off the stage washed over me. I opened my eyes, trying not to panic as they immediately went to Aiden again. He smiled widely and nodded, giving me the encouragement I needed to do this.

I lifted the microphone to my lips and started singing.

Just like the few times we'd rehearsed it, the ladies of the choir were immediately in sync and harmonizing with me as I sang Silent Night. The entire mall seemed to have gone quiet, not a screaming child or person talking for miles.

My hips began to sway gently with the music as I began walking across the stage, finally feeling in my element again.

Before I knew it, the song was over and led into the next in our set, Jingle Bell Rock—where the ladies made full use of the bells attached to their belts as they moved in time with the song. I smiled and did my best to keep from laughing so I could keep my composure and avoid messing up the words I was supposed to be singing.

We made it through O Come All Ye Faithful and White Christmas before ending with O Holy Night. This was the only song we hadn't rehearsed much together as a group, but I had been practicing it by myself while Aiden was at work.

It wasn't until I got close to the middle of the song that I noticed the ladies weren't singing as loudly as they should have been. It was almost as if the entire room had gone silent again. I closed my eyes and gave it everything I had as I belted out the last *fall on your knees*, hitting notes I'd never hit before and surprising myself with the amount of control I had while singing this song with more conviction than ever before.

Once I was done, I opened my eyes and found all eyes on me. I glanced nervously over my shoulder and found my mom wiping tears from her cheeks, as well as a few of the other ladies. Just then, clapping erupted all around me, and I could hear Aiden and Sam cheering from the very back.

The ladies all rushed up and wrapped their arms around me as I covered my mouth to keep from crying. Singing in front of thousands of fans was nothing compared to the rush I just got from performing in front of the people of Sugarplum Falls.

116

Twenty-Three
Aiden

"You were amazing," I said, picking Makayla up and spinning her in my arms as I hugged her tighter than ever. "Oh my God, Mak. Where in the world did you learn to sing like that?"

She giggled, the sound sending warm fuzzies straight to my heart as I set her down and made sure she wasn't too dizzy from all the spinning.

"I don't know," she admitted as a faint blush kissed her cheeks. "It just kinda came out of me, and I went with it. I'd been practicing that song by myself for a while now, but I didn't know I could do that."

I stepped back as more people came to congratulate her because I didn't want to continue to hog her.

"I'm going to head back to the shop to close for the day, but I'll meet you at the bar in an hour," Sam said, clapping my shoulder as I nodded.

Makayla didn't know it yet, but we had already started planning a party for tonight to celebrate the Sugarplum Sweetheart's win. Mainly it was Sam's idea, and I just ran with it because I wanted to shower Mak with as much attention as possible. Plus, the entire town was buzzing with electricity after her performance, and no one had been able to stop talking about it. It was no surprise when they were announced as the winners.

I stepped to the side to get out of the way while I checked my phone. Jackie confirmed that she had brought in extra help to get everything set up for tonight. There was a text message from Curtis acknowledging that we were having a party and that extra security would be provided there as well.

We had someone permanently stationed at my house, as well as at Jill's house, to make sure Kevin didn't get into either while they were gone. With security constantly following Makayla, it made it easier to be prepared if Kevin decided to make a move.

So far I had dinner covered by ordering plenty of pizza for everyone. Sam was going to pick up some wings on his way over, and Andi was bringing dessert. A few of the ladies from the church offered to bring some dishes as well, so I thanked them for their generosity and let them know Jackie would be there to help them set up when they were ready. Everyone was working on getting stuff handled while I was focused on Makayla and how happy she looked. I hadn't seen her smile like this in a long time, and deep down, I hoped it was enough to make her consider staying in Sugarplum Falls.

****

After Makayla got changed, we headed to the bar. I didn't tell her there was anything planned and hoped that no one had spoiled the surprise for her yet. While Sugarplum Falls loved a good party, they were also the worst secret keepers when it came to parties.

By the time we got there, the parking lot was already halfway full, which immediately caught Makayla's attention.

"What's going on?" she asked as she unbuckled and reached for the door handle.

"You'll see."

I hopped out of the truck and rushed around to help her out. I could tell she was nervous but loved that she trusted me enough to go inside.

I opened the door and held it for her, gently placing my hand on her lower back to guide her in as everyone yelled *surprise*.

She jumped back, her hands flying to her mouth as she looked around.

"Oh my gosh! What is all of this?"

"It's a celebration," I said, my voice low in her ear as everyone cheered her name. "You led the Sugarplum Sweethearts to victory today, and everyone wanted to have a party to celebrate."

She turned and looked at me, a smile on her beautiful face.

"This is too much," she said with a soft laugh. "If you keep throwing parties for me, I might not ever leave."

I swallowed hard, trying to get past the lump forming in my throat as hope rose to the surface. I would go broke throwing parties for her every day if that's what it took to get her to stay.

We made our way inside, everyone lining up to take their

turn hugging and congratulating her again. It was nice to see how easily everyone welcomed her back but also to see how receptive she was to all of the attention. Even though Makayla was a famous superstar who could sell out a tour within hours, she was still the same humble girl I fell in love with all those years ago.

Twenty-Four
Makayla

Between the beer and all of the food everyone had contributed to the party, I was beyond full. Sugar Faced Bar filled up faster than expected, so Aiden made sure to have Tony inside with a few other guys from my security detail while Patrick watched the outside with his team. There were also complete teams monitoring Aiden and my mom's house. It felt like the population in Sugarplum Falls had doubled in the past few days, and that was just from the added security that had been sent in to protect me.

I hadn't heard from Kevin since his call the other day. Curtis tried tracking his phone, but Tony ended up finding it in a trashcan inside the mall, which meant we had no way of knowing where he was anymore. Not only that, it had been registered to a bogus name, which made them doubt it was even his phone, to begin with. The Sugarplum Falls sheriff's department had joined forces with my security team to try to find him, but everyone was coming up empty. I wasn't going to let any of that bother me tonight because I was still riding the high of helping the Sugarplum Sweethearts win the caroling competition.

"Do you want another beer?" Sam asked, nodding to the empty mug in my hand.

"No, thank you. I've had enough for tonight."

He nodded and made his way up to the bar where Aiden was currently talking to Jackie. They scanned the room, and she nodded before I felt his eyes land on me. I gave a nervous smile and finger wave, already knowing they were talking about me.

Aiden had set up karaoke again, so I grabbed one of the papers that were sitting out by the basket and wrote down a song before tossing it in with the others. So far, it had been a fun night of laughing and dancing with people who had quickly gone from acquaintances I barely remembered to friends I couldn't get enough of.

I sat on one of the barstools off in the corner of the room, swinging my feet and dancing as my mom and Brock did a duet of *You're The One That I Want* from Grease. I had met him a few times since I'd been in town and could see why my mom loved him so much. He was one of the nicest guys I had ever met, and it warmed my heart to see how happy he made her.

"Are you having a good time?" Aiden asked, startling me as he snuck up beside me.

I turned and grinned at him, the beer making me a little more buzzed than I thought.

"The best."

The DJ waited for my mom to hand over her microphone before reaching into the basket and tossing the papers around before pulling one out.

"Alright folks, up next, we have Makayla and Aiden singing Hakuna Matata."

I looked up in time to see his eyebrows shoot up to his forehead as he shook his head no.

"Makayla," he warned as I hopped off my barstool and grabbed his hand to drag him with me.

The only problem was that he didn't budge.

Damn, he's really strong. Strong enough to do some man-handling with me later tonight if I was lucky.

"No way, Mak."

"Come on," I whined, still pulling with all of my might.

"That song?"

"What?" I shrugged, playing innocent. "It means no worries."

"You know I don't sing."

"But you used to."

"That was a long time ago," he countered, finally showing me some mercy as his feet moved.

"Yeah, and it was fun. You know how much we loved doing this song."

"When we were like ten." His eyebrow continued to arch at me, sending shivers across my skin.

I stopped and sighed heavily.

"Fine."

"Fine, as in you won't make me sing?" he asked with a hint of a smile.

I grinned at the DJ and accepted the two cordless mics he handed me.

"No, *fine* as in you can sing Timon's part this time, and I'll do Pumba."

He let his head fall as he shook his head.

"I don't know why I let you talk me into this shit," he said with a genuine smile this time.

"Because you love me," I replied, feeling the weight of my words the second I said them.

"That I do." His words were quiet but still loud enough for me to hear.

We took the stage and I grinned like a fool as everyone cheered and went wild that Aiden was going to sing.

Once the music started, I felt him nudge me with his elbow as he gave me a nod. His way of saying we could sing the song the way we always did.

I began singing Timon's part, trying not to laugh as Aiden immediately sank into Pumba's part. The crowd went wild again, celebrating this song more than anything anyone else had sung tonight.

It wasn't until we got to the part when Pumba sings about when he was a young warthog that I burst out laughing as Aiden did his best opera impression that matched that of the song. We played into the enthusiasm of the crowd, bringing a full performance with theatrics and everything.

Once the song was over, we bowed and smiled as everyone continued to applaud. We moved out of the way after giving the microphones back, and I felt Aiden's hand guide me to the side.

"Thanks for singing that with me," I said, already feeling

out of breath from the way he was looking at me.

"There's nothing I wouldn't do for you, Mak."

Then he wrapped an arm around my waist as he slightly dipped me, his mouth crashing down over mine.

This time, everyone was cheering again, but not because someone was on stage singing. They were literally cheering for us making out in a crowded bar packed full of some of the best people I'd ever met.

126

Twenty-Five
Aiden

The bar started dying down around midnight with most of the older crowd heading home after the karaoke ended. Makayla was in the middle of the room, dancing with Andi and Jasmin as they laughed and had a great time.

I talked with Jackie to see what time she wanted to go home since I was closing up tonight. Some of the security had cleared out as well, likely watching the cameras at both houses to make sure Jill got home safely. I didn't worry as much about her since Brock was home tonight, but it was still better to keep an eye on everything until Kevin made his whereabouts known.

"Hey," I said, pulling Makayla into my arms as the song ended and the girls cleared the dance floor. "I'm staying to close up tonight, but I can ask Tony to take you home whenever you're ready."

"Is it okay if I stay with you and have *you* take me home?"

She wasn't as buzzed as she was earlier, but definitely more relaxed than I had seen her in a while. It could be because of all the fucking we did last night or possibly because the stress of the competition was officially off of her shoulders. Either way, I loved this relaxed version of her.

"That's fine with me, but I don't want you to be bored

staying here while I wait for everyone to clear out."

"I honestly don't mind. Heck, you can even put me to work cleaning tables or something."

"I appreciate the offer, but that's what I pay those guys to do." I nodded toward the two bussers who were clearing the last of the tables.

Typically, I would stay open until two in the morning, but since it was already pretty empty, I couldn't imagine we would be open too much longer.

"We're going to get going," Andi said, interrupting to give both of us a hug. "Zach's waiting outside to give us a ride, but do you need any help cleaning up before we go?"

"Na, we got it but thank you. Be safe getting home."

Andi nodded and locked arms with Jasmin as they headed out into the cold winter air.

"You guys can go ahead and take off," I called out to the bussers. "Finish those and then head out with Jackie."

They nodded, taking the last of the dirty glasses to the kitchen where Jackie was finishing up, leaving Makayla and me alone in the bar. I filled a glass with ice water and set it on the bar in front of her as she climbed up onto the barstool. I knew she was probably tired from how early we'd gotten up and with it being a long day, but she didn't let it show.

Jackie came out a few minutes later with the guys, waving as they left.

"Did you have fun tonight?" I asked Makayla as I began closing out the register.

"I did. But then again, I always have fun when I'm here. You have an amazing place to hang out. I can see why it's so popular here."

"Alcohol is what makes it so popular," I teased, winking at her over my shoulder.

"I'm sure that helps, but seriously, people come here because it's a great atmosphere. Between the karaoke and the dancing, there's always something fun to do."

"Do you go out a lot in LA?"

She shook her head and took a long sip of her water.

"Not unless I have to. Occasionally, there will be a social event I need to attend, but it's usually at stuffy bars with a dress code and stuck-up people. Nothing like this."

"That sucks. You don't ever just go out for fun with friends?"

"What friends?" She snorted and tried to play it off as a joke, but I immediately noticed the sadness that washed over her face.

I stopped what I was doing and turned around to face her. My arms crossed over my chest to keep from reaching out to touch her.

"Are you happy, Mak?"

She blinked quickly as she looked away and took another drink.

"Yeah. Of course I am. Why wouldn't I be? I have the job I've always wanted. I'm living in a big city, and I get to travel the world."

I walked around the bar and stood in front of her as I spun her seat around.

"Be honest. It's just us. You don't have to say what you think I want to hear. I want the truth. Are you happy?"

Her shoulders fell as the smile she tried plastering to her face vanished.

"I used to be. Or at least I thought I was."

"What made you change your mind?"

I lifted her chin with my finger so she would look at me.

"You."

My heart skipped a beat as I stepped closer to her, needing to feel her body next to mine.

"What about me?"

"You made me realize how unhappy I've been by showing me how happy I am here. I got so caught up in what I thought I should be with my music and touring the world, but I never stopped to question if I was truly happy until now."

I cupped the back of her head and lowered my mouth to hers.

Her hands immediately locked behind my neck as she deepened the kiss. I could already feel her body responding to my touch and loved it.

I slid my hands down and lifted her from the barstool, smiling when she locked her legs around my waist. Our mouths continued to devour each other as I set her on top of the bar and lifted her shirt over her head.

Pebbled nipples greeted me through the thin fabric of her black lace bra, begging to be sucked. I quickly unclasped the back of her bra, releasing them as I leaned in and pulled one into my mouth. Makayla grabbed a fistful of hair and leaned back, allowing me full access as I massaged the other while continuing to torture her nipple with gentle bites and hard sucking.

My cock strained against my jeans as she shifted against my face.

"I want you to fuck me, Aiden," she panted. "Now."

I nodded, fully on board with this decision.

I picked her up and lowered her feet to the floor, grinning when she started pulling down her leggings and panties, stopping when they reached her knees.

"Bend over the barstool," I instructed as I unzipped my jeans and pulled my cock out.

She did as I asked, legs spread as far as she could with the fabric restraining her. At this angle, I had the perfect view of her pussy which was glistening and ready for me.

I lined up at her entrance, gently swiping a finger through her folds to make sure she was ready.

"Ahh," she cried out, lifting her ass higher to allow me better access.

"Fuck, baby. You're so wet for me."

She nodded, looking over her shoulder at me.

"You always make me wet. Especially when you suck my nipples like that."

I smirked and then slapped her ass playfully before pushing inside.

Her back arched as she pushed back against me, her pussy wrapped so tightly around my cock.

I hissed out another breath as I bit down on my lower lip to try to keep from coming. It was almost impossible with Makayla because she felt so incredible—especially without a condom. I hadn't been lying when I said I wanted to knock her up and have her carry my children. Nothing turned me on more than her being pregnant with my baby.

I pulled out, smiling at how wet my cock was from her arousal and gripped her hips tightly as I slammed back inside her.

She cried out the most beautiful moan as I did it again.

I knew she loved this as much as I did and could feel her getting wetter by the second.

"Make yourself come, baby," I coaxed, knowing I couldn't reach her clit as easily in this position. The best I could do was angle my dick to hit her g-spot, but I wanted to make sure she came good and hard.

She adjusted slightly as she reached down and began rubbing herself.

"Oh my God, Aiden," she moaned as I plowed into her over and over as she brought herself to climax.

Her pussy spasming around my cock was all it took for me to unload inside of her, my balls tightening as I came harder than ever before.

We stood there for a moment, both catching our breath

before I slowly pulled out of her. I grabbed a couple of napkins from the counter and wiped myself off before debating on whether to clean her up as well.

"Leave it," she said, already reading my mind as she pulled up her leggings and smiled. "I want to feel you leaking out of me."

I shook my head and grinned, knowing she was going to be the death of me.

134

Twenty-Six
Makayla

I'd never been in a parade before, let alone on a float. Add on the extra pressure of being the very first float in the parade, as well as being the *only* person on the stage, and my nerves were at an all-time high. The ladies of the Sugarplum Sweethearts were seated around the stage, facing out toward the crowd as they tossed candy canes while I sang.

I thought it was cute that we all wore matching ugly sweaters, especially since it was freezing outside. There were reports that a big snowstorm was heading in, but thankfully it was dry this morning.

I considered sitting on the chair they'd provided for me on the stage, but it felt too much like being a queen sitting on her throne. Thankfully, the float moved so slowly that I didn't have to worry about keeping my balance as I walked around, making sure I took turns on which side of the street I faced so everyone could see me.

The songs today were more fun and upbeat which had the kids in the crowd smiling. I couldn't stop thinking about what Aiden had said about wanting to knock me up. I hadn't given much thought to my future once my music career started, but now was as good a time as any to start thinking about it. I was already twenty-eight and didn't want to wait too long before deciding whether or not I wanted to start a family. These things took time, and if I didn't stop and start planning now, I might miss the opportunity. My career was at its peak, and I had another world tour lined up, which meant I would be thirty by the time I finished.

I looked ahead, curious to see how far the parade went and was surprised to see that the street continued to be lined up with people for miles ahead of us. Aiden wasn't lying when he said that people came from all over to be here for Frosty Fest, which was good for business in Sugarplum Falls.

The music stopped after the last song ended, and I wondered if that was it for the singing portion of the parade. I smiled and waved at everyone, curious about what else I was supposed to do since we still had a ways to go.

Then, just as suddenly as the music stopped, it started again.

I smiled when I recognized the tune of O Holy Night and caught my mom's eye as she looked up at me.

"They all wanted a repeat of yesterday's performance," she yelled up to me, trying to be heard over the gust of wind that whipped between us.

I nodded and took a deep breath, hoping I could do it as well as I had yesterday.

I began singing, closing my eyes as I allowed the music and words to consume me. Singing was what always calmed me, and being the center of attention was something I was used to. But nothing could stop that rush of adrenaline I felt every time I heard the people of Sugarplum Falls cheer for me.

By the time the parade was over, I was shivering and in desperate need of something warm to drink. I rushed into the mall as my mom stayed behind to talk with the ladies. Apparently, they were helping out with the rest of Frosty Fest and needed to check in with Jasmin to see where she wanted them.

I made my way through the mall, grinning ear to ear as I took in the massive displays in front of me. There were booths lined up as far as I could see with vendors I hadn't heard of before. In the middle of everything was the same stage we had performed on yesterday that was now transformed into the North Pole. Elves were rushing around setting up the last few details before Santa and Mrs. Claus came out to take pictures with the kids.

"Where are you headed?" Aiden asked, coming up beside me and startling me.

"You scared the shit out of me," I said with a laugh, holding my hand over the fuzzy ornament on my sweater.

"Sorry. I thought you heard me calling your name."

"Nope. I was lost in thought, taking this all in while searching for coffee."

"Sam has a booth set up in the food court if you want a latte."

"Seriously? That's pretty awesome."

"Yeah, he does killer business during Frosty Fest. His assistant manager runs the shop while he runs things here. They hire extra help a few months before because it gets that busy."

"Wow. He's doing amazing things for himself." I looked around at the lines forming around the booths and shook my head. "You all are. I cannot believe this. It's insane how many people are here."

"Frosty Fest is a huge deal. Everyone in town shows up for it. We also make sure to help out those who are working it so they have time to go enjoy it as well. There's a lot of community support here, but a lot of the traffic today is people coming from out of town. We've grown so much in the past five years, but I worry that we're already to the point that we're going to outgrow the space again. Jasmin does a great job managing everything and redirecting traffic so all of the vendors stay busy, but it's getting to the point where she's going to have to look for a new venue to accommodate everyone."

"I can imagine. I don't think I've seen this many people in a mall before."

"Why don't we get you some coffee, and then we can look around?"

"I'd like that. Thank you." I locked my arm in his and allowed him to lead the way as I soaked up the feeling of contentment that was radiating through me.

Twenty-Seven
Aiden

Shopping with Makayla at Frosty Fest was fun, but I couldn't stop worrying about the possibility of Kevin making a move today. Without knowing what he looked like and so many people visiting from out of town, he could easily get close to her.

Tony and Patrick did their best to blend in as they followed right behind us, but everyone in town knew they were there for Mak. I knew there were at least twenty other security guys dispersed throughout the mall, but I didn't know who they were or what they looked like. We were supposed to just carry on as if there was nothing to worry about, which was incredibly hard to do.

This morning during the parade, I spotted at least one security guard every few feet as they kept an eye on Makayla. Not only was her team present, but the Sugarplum Falls Sherrif's department was there as well. I had expected the heavy police presence to make people nervous, but everyone was so caught up in the charm of Frosty Fest that they didn't seem to notice.

"I need to make a pitstop real quick," Makayla said, pointing to a store across from us. "By myself." She held her hand up and pressed it against my chest to keep me from going with her.

I frowned and was about to object when Tony caught my eye and gave me a subtle nod.

"I'll be fine. I promise. I'm sure Tony and Patrick don't mind doing some shopping with me, do you guys?" She turned and smiled at them over her shoulder.

"No, ma'am," Patrick said, standing straight and rigid as his eyes scanned the room for any signs of a threat.

"I told you to stop calling me ma'am. You make me feel old." She playfully swatted at his arm, but he didn't respond.

"Come on, let's go shopping. I'll meet you in the food court in half an hour?"

"Sure. Sounds good." I sighed heavily and shoved a hand through my hair, hating that she was going off on her own. Yes, technically, she had her security team with her, but *I* wasn't there, and that made me feel uneasy.

I watched as she walked to the store and gave me a quick wave before heading inside. My jaw hurt from how tight I was grinding it, so I forced myself to turn around and head back toward the food court so I could keep an eye on things until Makayla got there.

The makeshift aisles between the booths were packed as I tried to make my way through. I was almost out of the maze when I heard someone call my name. I turned around and found Hadley waving at me from the Sugarplum Gifts booth.

"Hey, Hadley. What's up?"

"I am so sorry to bother you, but I really need the restroom, and my help hasn't arrived yet. Is there any way you can watch the booth for a few minutes while I run real quick?"

"Absolutely. Take your time."

"Thank you! You can let people know I'll be back in a minute to ring them up if anyone wants to buy something. Santa and Mrs. Claus just got on stage, so a lot of people took off to get in line for that, so I figured now was my chance."

"You got it."

She smiled and ducked out the back of the booth, rushing to the restroom.

I was relieved there was no one in line because I had no idea what I would even say. I was used to talking to people about drinks and what kind of whiskey I liked, not what these delicate-looking ornaments were made out of.

I shoved my hands in my pockets and looked around, wondering if I would even know Kevin if I saw him. Would he be obvious by looking suspicious, or would he try to blend in with the tourists and pretend to shop while looking for Makayla?

"Hi," a woman said, coming up to the booth and startling me.

"Good morning." I offered her a smile, which was returned before she started looking at the selection of jewelry in a locked display case. "These bracelets are beautiful. Do you know what they're made out of?"

I leaned in closer to take a look, frowning when I realized that I had no clue. I also didn't have the key, so I couldn't open the box to take one out to see.

"I'm sorry, I don't. I'm just covering for Hadley. She

should be back in a few minutes and can answer that for you better than I can."

"No worries. Thank you." She smiled again and moved to the other side of the booth, where the ornaments were on display.

I sighed and felt relieved when Hadley slipped in beside me.

"I'm back," she said, smiling at the woman who was still shopping the ornaments.

"She was curious what the bracelets were made out of," I said, nodding to the display case.

"They're all 24-karat gold," Hadley explained, grabbing a key and unlocking the case. She pulled out one that was rose gold and had a heart with a diamond in the middle that rested on top of three solid bands.

"Umm, can I see that one?" I asked nervously, hoping it wasn't the one the lady was wanting.

Hadley smiled and handed it to me while the woman turned her attention to the display case and pointed to another bracelet.

My heart leaped into my chest as a wave of excitement rushed over me as I pictured Makayla wearing this. I'd seen her wear jewelry before and knew rose gold was her favorite.

"Can I get this?" I asked Hadley once she was done helping her customer.

"Of course. Let me grab a box for it real quick."

She reached under the table and grabbed what she needed before ringing it up and giving me my total. I handed her my credit card and looked around for Makayla, unsure how much time had passed while I was distracted by the bracelet.

"She's going to love it," Hadley said, smiling as she tucked the black box inside a small gift bag and handed it to me.

I felt my cheeks flame with heat as I lowered my eyes and took it from her.

"Thanks, Hadley. I hope so."

I gave her a quick hug and then snuck out of the booth as a new wave of customers approached.

Twenty-Eight
Makayla

"Do you think he'll like this?" I asked, holding up a black knit sweater for Tony and Patrick to see.

"It's whatever you like, ma'am," Patrick said, barely looking at the garment as he scanned the room again.

"What do you think, Tony?"

His attention appeared to be on me, but my guess was that he was also scanning the room behind me.

"I think he has enough sweaters," he said gruffly, giving me his full attention for one second before looking past me.

"You guys are no help," I grumbled, putting the sweater back on the rack and shuffling the stuff in my basket so it wasn't so heavy on my arm.

So far, I'd managed to get a few things for my mom even though I'd already shipped her gifts before I came out here. I didn't want to risk them getting lost or damaged on the flight, and I was too lazy to want to deal with getting someone to help me carry all of my stuff from baggage claim to my rental car.

I'd also picked up a few things for myself but was struggling with what to get Aiden. We hadn't discussed whether we were exchanging gifts, but since we seemed to be a couple again, I didn't want to *not* get him anything. Plus, it was supposed to be fun shopping for your loved ones—though I wasn't currently having any fun as everything seemed to be a flop.

I walked down the main aisle and stopped when I spotted a set of skull-shaped whiskey glasses. I knew that Aiden loved a good whiskey, and when I was snooping through his stuff at home, I noticed he only had one glass. I grabbed a set of glasses and made sure to balance them in the basket so they didn't fall out, then reached for the matching decanter. It was almost within reach when I felt the basket shift and the glasses slip out the side.

Tony's reflexes were quicker than I could have anticipated as his hand shot out and grabbed them before they hit the floor.

"Woah," I said, genuinely impressed. "Nice catch."

"Thank you." He held the glasses under his arm and locked his hands in front of him as he scanned the room again. "Those are a much better gift."

"Right? He'll love them!" I grabbed the decanter and went to add it to the basket when Patrick extended his hand and took it.

I smiled at him but rolled my eyes when he didn't see it because he was looking everywhere else.

"I want to get him a bottle of whiskey to go with it, but we can do that on the way home. I'll tell him you guys are giving me a ride so the surprise doesn't get ruined."

"Yes, ma'am," Patrick said.

"Patrick, I love you and it's less than a week until Christmas, so I don't want to hurt you. But I swear, if you call me *ma'am* one more time," I warned, giving him the best glare I could.

"Got it, ma—"

I arched an eyebrow and then smiled when he stopped himself.

"Alright, I think I'm all set. We can go pay real quick, then I'll text Aiden to let him know I'm heading to the food court."

Neither of them answered but followed me as I headed to the registers. I paid for my stuff and thankfully, the cashier was kind enough to double bag Aiden's gift so he couldn't tell what it was. I was relieved to have most of my shopping done, but that didn't mean I was done with Frosty Fest. There were still a handful of vendor booths I hadn't gotten to yet, which meant my day of fun was just starting.

Twenty-Nine
Aiden

It was after seven by the time Makayla got home. We left Frosty Fest around five, but she insisted on getting a ride home with Tony and Patrick because she had a few errands to run that I couldn't be part of. That worked for me since I needed time to wrap her gifts while she was gone.

In addition to the bracelet, I'd also gone a little crazy and bought everything she touched at the different vendors we visited in the mall. I would make up an excuse about needing to go do something and leave her with Tony and Patrick while I ran back to grab handfuls of stuff from different booths. She had no idea what I was doing—or at least I hoped she didn't, which made it that much more fun to shop for her.

It felt like she might have been relieved to have a break from me every now and then as well, but I tried not to take it personally.

By the time she got home, dinner was almost ready. I helped her inside as Tony and Patrick carried bags and bags full of stuff inside for her.

"Do I want to know why you bought the entire store at Waldon's?" I asked, arching an eyebrow as I studied the bags in their hands.

"I needed supplies." She shrugged, sliding her purse off and hanging it on the coat rack by the door. "And then I decided to take some time to check the store out. Do you know how much stuff they have in there?"

"I do." I nodded, smiling. "People can spend hours in there, apparently." I winked to let her know I was just teasing.

"You seriously could. I had to stop myself because I was worried we would run out of room in the rental car. Plus, Patrick seemed like he was getting grumpy, so I figured we should call it a day. But I finished all of my Christmas shopping and got some fun stuff as well. Where do you want us to put all of this so you won't be nosey and go through it?"

"In the office is fine," I said, heading to the oven to pull the pizza out. "And I would never do that."

"You would too," she countered as she headed down the hallway and into the office.

"That was one time," I hollered back, setting the pizza pan on the stove. "And I was seven."

"Still. Once a snoop, always a snoop."

She came into the kitchen wearing a smile and hiding a bag behind her back.

"Have a good night, guys," she called out over her shoulder as Tony and Patrick left, never taking her eyes off me.

"What do you have behind your back?"

"A little present for you."

"It's not Christmas yet."

"It's not a Christmas gift."

I leaned to the side, trying to see where the bag was from.

"Nope. No cheating."

"If it's my present, then it's not cheating if I try to see what it is."

"It's cheating if I say it's cheating. Now close your eyes and hold out your hands."

I narrowed my eyes at her, then did as she asked.

She pulled something out of the bag and placed it in my hands. It was light, but there was a crinkling sound, like that of tissue paper.

"Okay, open your eyes."

I opened them slowly and stared at the red tissue paper in my hands. I gave her a questioning look so I didn't get in trouble for trying to open it if she wasn't ready.

"Go ahead," she said with a sexy smile.

I pulled the tissue paper back and held up a piece of red lingerie that had a thin strip of white fur that lined the top of where the bra cups should go. Only they weren't there, which meant her breasts would be on full display and easily accessible in this.

I looked up at her and found her chewing her nails nervously as she watched me.

It was sexy as hell and I couldn't wait to see it on her as I held it up and noticed that it had crotchless panties as well.

"Very nice," I said, pressing the silky fabric against my

body as I smirked at her. "But I don't think it'll fit me."

"You dork, it's for *me* to wear for *you*," she replied, swatting at my arm as she tried to get it back.

"Well then, I guess you better go put it on."

"But the pizza is ready," she objected, looking from me to the pan sitting on the stove. "Plus, I have to wash it first. I thought maybe I could wear it for you on Christmas Eve."

"You can't show me something sexy like that and then expect me to wait that long for it," I whined, not loving where this was going.

"Well," she said with a heavy sigh, resting her hands on my shoulders. "I guess I'll just have to make it up to you after dinner with a blow job on the couch."

My eyebrows shot up in surprise as a wicked smile crossed my face.

"You sure do know how to negotiate."

She leaned in and kissed the tip of my nose before taking the lingerie and stuffing it back into the bag. I was disappointed I wouldn't get to see her in it right away, but I was already looking forward to the blow job tonight, as well as the fact that she was planning to spend Christmas Eve with me.

Thirty
Makayla

The days leading up to Christmas flew by, and before I knew it, it was already Christmas Eve. Aiden had gone in to work early this morning, which was nice because I had a whole night planned for us and didn't want to have any interruptions.

I'd spent the morning wrapping the last of the Christmas gifts I'd purchased throughout the week. Who knew shopping in Sugarplum Falls could be so fun? Or maybe it was just that I liked how there was so much handmade stuff here, and I loved supporting local artisans.

My mom and I were supposed to be having lunch today, but I was waiting for her to get home before I headed over. Something felt off, but I tried to shake the feeling as I waited for her to text me to say that she was ready.

I did a load of laundry, making sure everything I needed for tonight was ready. Aiden hadn't stopped talking about the lingerie I had purchased, so I went out and bought more. It was weird because I didn't have a set time that I would be in Sugarplum Falls, and we both knew that. We'd talked about what would happen when I had to go back to LA, and we promised that we would find a way to make a long-distance relationship work.

My phone dinged with a new text message, so I picked it up, hoping it was my mom.

Aiden: Just wanted to say how much I miss you, and I can't wait to see you when I get home.

A grin spread across my cheeks, making them hurt from how big it was.

Me: I can't wait to see you too.

Aiden: Aren't you supposed to be meeting your mom for lunch?

Me: Yeah. I'm just waiting for her to get home.

Just then, another text message came through.

Mom: I'm home.

It still felt weird to be going to her house for lunch instead of Brock's since that's where she had been staying. But she wanted to make lunch there since we had spent so many holidays together in that house. It didn't bother me any since we had an entire security team watching everything, and deep down, it felt nice to have something that felt familiar and brought the comfort I'd remembered when I was little.

Me: Okay, I'm on my way.

I grabbed my purse from the table and sent a text back to Aiden.

Me: My mom just got home, so I'm heading over there now. See you later!

Aiden: Have fun. I'll see you tonight. Love you.

Me: I love you too.

I shoved my phone into my pocket and opened the door,

smiling when I saw Tony waiting for me.

"Perfect timing," I said, pulling the door closed behind me and locking it. He smiled and walked behind me as I headed to the car where Patrick was already inside. It felt weird having my security detail double as my chauffeurs, but it worked. This was just another means to ensure my safety, which I was fine with.

The drive to my mom's house was quick, as was everything in Sugarplum Falls.

Before I was allowed to get out of the house, Tony and Patrick checked the cameras for any signs of trouble before Tony got out and escorted me to the front door.

I knocked, not bothering to look for my keys. A few seconds later, my mom answered the door, and my stomach immediately dropped.

"Mom, what's wrong?" I asked, stepping inside and reaching for her.

She was pale and looked like she had seen a ghost.

"Nothing, dear. Everything is fine. Did you bring the fruit cake?"

I pulled my brows together in confusion as I stared at her. What in the world was she talking about? *Fruit cake? When had we ever eaten fruit cake together?*

Her eyes widened, almost as if pleading with me.

"Shoot. I totally forgot to grab it. Why don't you run with me to the store?" I offered, completely worried now as I reached for her hand. She pulled away quickly, making the hairs on my arm stand straight.

"Oh, no. I can't do that. I need to stay here and watch the turkey in the oven."

I glanced past her, noticing the oven wasn't on, nor was there the familiar smell of one cooking.

"Okay. It's fine. I can go real quick and come back." I leaned in to hug her and whispered quietly in her ear. "Mom, you're scaring me. What's going on."

"Leave now," she whispered, pushing me away with tears in her eyes.

My blood turned cold as I noticed a small cut above her eyebrow.

"Where's Brock?" I whispered, forgetting that he was supposed to be joining us. Why hadn't he protected her from whatever was going on?

Tony stood at my side, and I noticed the moment his hand reached for his holster. His body angled close to mine as his eyes constantly scanned the room.

"He had to go to work today."

Something was wrong. Very, very wrong. Brock had the day off, which was why we were having lunch together.

"Okay. I'll go get the fruit cake, and then we can figure out lunch when I get back."

I turned and faced Tony, my eyes wide and brimming with tears. He gave me a subtle nod, confirming he knew something was wrong as well. He leaned his head to his shoulder and spoke quietly into the microphone.

Within seconds, the front door flew open, and Patrick

grabbed me, moving me to the kitchen before a handful of security guys rushed through the house. I reached for my mom, thankful when one of them guided her to me before sweeping the house.

"Drop your weapon now!" Tony yelled from the back of the house.

I closed my eyes and hugged my mom, terrified over what was happening.

There was a heavy thud and then a few other loud noises as more security rushed inside.

Patrick stood in front of me and my mom with his gun drawn and aimed in front of him.

A few minutes later, Tony came out with a man I'd seen plenty of times before handcuffed in front of him.

"Sean?" I asked, stepping out from behind Patrick before his body immediately blocked mine again. I squinted to try to see better, barely recognizing him with the full beard and long, shaggy hair.

"Stand back," Patrick commanded, his weapon still aimed as Tony and Sean moved through the living room.

"What in the world is going on? Sean isn't a threat. He runs my fan club," I insisted, trying to get past Patrick so I could explain to them that they had the wrong guy.

But then it immediately hit me that there wasn't any reason for Sean to be in my mother's house.

It had been a while since I'd seen Sean, given that he moved two years ago and was now working remotely. Curtis took over managing him, which meant there wasn't a need for me to be involved anymore. My heart sank when I realized that my issues with a stalker started shortly after Sean had left.

The rest of the security team came out, two of them assisting Brock, who had a bloody face. They helped him to the recliner and then stood guard beside him.

I covered my mouth and looked up at Sean with more tears filling my eyes.

"They weren't going to let us be together," he said, shaking his head. "I was your biggest fan, and you never even noticed. You don't care about your fans or anyone other than yourself."

"That's not true," I objected, my mind racing as I struggled to put all the pieces together of what was happening.

"It is, and you know it. I've done everything for you, Makayla. Everything!" he shouted, making me jump back behind Patrick. "You're so caught up in yourself that you didn't even see that I was in love with you. I tried to tell you, but you blew me off so many times. I didn't get your attention until I pretended to be someone else."

"Kevin," I whispered, shaking my head, the reality of it sinking in.

"Yeah. And even then, he still wasn't good enough for you. You had to come back to this hell hole and crawl back to your stupid ex-boyfriend. He didn't care enough to make things work the first time. What makes you think he will now?"

"That's enough out of you," Tony said, shoving him forward as the sheriff took him into custody.

"I love you, Makayla! One way or another, I will be with you!"

His voice floated outside before the door slammed shut. Patrick secured his weapon in its holster and then turned to me and my mom.

"Are you two alright?"

"Yeah," I said, nodding my head, though I was pretty shaken up. "She has a cut on her head, so someone needs to tend to that."

"We have medics on the way," one of the officers from the sheriff's department answered.

I followed my mom over to the couch and sat down as officers and my security team rushed around us. They were securing the scene and collecting evidence, so we sat there, out of the way. Brock sat across from us, holding a towel against his forehead where a massive cut was bleeding.

"I am so sorry," I said with a sob. "I didn't mean for any of this to happen."

"This isn't your fault, honey," my mom assured me, squeezing my hand gently.

"Yes, it is. If it weren't for me, Kev—Sean wouldn't have come here and hurt you guys. I mean, look at poor Brock. Are you sure we can't do something for you until the paramedics get here? That looks pretty bad."

"I'm fine," he said, waving me off. "I told them I could suture it myself in the bathroom, but they refused to let me. So now I'm just applying pressure to stop the bleeding until someone else can do it for me. It's honestly not as bad as it looks. A couple of stitches, and I'll be back to normal."

"How did he even get in here?" I asked, turning to where Patrick was talking to the other guys on my security detail with an iPad in front of them.

"He was able to disable the cameras somehow. That's why no one saw him enter the house. The guys watching the house were monitoring the front and back door since the cameras should have caught any motion along the side of the house. It appears he came in through a window in the guest room."

"Where I was supposed to be staying," I said quietly. "I left the stupid window open because I was hot that first night I got here. I closed it but didn't bother to lock it because it always sticks, and I didn't want it to wake you up. Plus, there's never any crime in Sugarplum Falls." I rubbed my hands over my eyes and shook my head in frustration.

"You didn't know any of this was going to happen," my mom continued, rubbing my back soothingly. "We all tried to be as prepared as possible, but at least now they caught him. He can't bother you anymore, Makayla. All of that is over now."

I lifted my head and let my shoulders fall as I exhaled a heavy breath. Just then, Aiden came flying through the door, eyes wide as he searched the room for me.

"I'm fine," I said, immediately pulling his attention to me.

He rushed over and sat on the couch beside me, squeezing into the little space left between me and the armrest.

"I came as soon as I heard," he said, rubbing his thumb lightly over my cheek. "I can't believe this happened."

"I can't believe it's been Sean the whole time," I replied, leaning against the cushion behind me. "He's been running my fan club for the past *five years*. How could I have been so blind?"

"You weren't blind. You just didn't have any reason to suspect him." Aiden's eyes were soft as they looked into mine. "People often show us what they want us to see."

"True, but I feel like so much of this could have been prevented if I was more involved or less distracted."

"You hired someone to manage your fan club because you didn't have the time to," my mother softly reminded me. "That's a normal thing to do, especially in your line of business. If you were busy taking care of everything, you'd have no time to record new music, no time to tour. Delegation was created for a reason."

"Your mom is right," Brock said. "There was no way you could have seen this coming. Don't be so hard on yourself."

I allowed Aiden to pull me into his side and hold me as Patrick updated everyone on what was happening. No one on my security team had recognized him since he wasn't considered a threat. It also helped him stay mixed in with the tourists because he wasn't at the LA office anymore and was now working remotely.

I talked to Curtis, and he gave me some updates as well, including Sean's immediate termination and the request he'd sent to collect the company computer he had been given when he moved. All in all, the good news was that this part was over. I didn't have to keep watching over my shoulders, and even though it was already Christmas Eve, I had hope that my security detail could all get home to their families for Christmas.

BLAME IT ON THE CAROLS

Thirty-One
Aiden

"We don't have to do anything tonight," I called to Makayla, who insisted on getting ready in the bathroom for whatever she had planned before all of the Kevin/Sean stuff happened.

"I want to. Now shut up and get ready for me."

"How do you want me to get ready if I don't know what's happening?"

"Take your pants off and close your eyes."

I nodded my head, though she couldn't see me from the bathroom. I stood up and took off my jeans, tossing them to the chair as I resumed my position on the couch.

"Are your eyes closed?" she asked, the sound of heels clicking against the tile floor.

"They are now," I answered, closing them and leaning my head against the cushion behind me.

The sweet scent of her perfume floated in the air around us as I felt her straddle me. It sucked having my eyes closed because I could tell from the fishnet stockings I felt when I touched her legs that I definitely wanted to see whatever she was wearing.

She guided my hands up her thighs and then lowered one between her legs, where I was immediately greeted with warmth.

"Fuck, Mak," I moaned, my fingers desperately trying to slide between her wet slit before she moved my hand away.

"Keep your eyes closed," she warned as they fluttered slightly.

Then she guided my hands up her stomach, the silky softness of the fabric pleasant to touch before I felt the warmth of her skin as a pebbled nipple brushed against my finger.

She was wearing the lingerie she promised she would wear tonight and I couldn't wait to actually see it.

"You know this is pure torture, right?"

"Relax, I'll let you look in a minute," she replied with a soft laugh. "I can already feel you getting hard beneath me and I promise I'll be taking care of that here in a minute."

My fingers rolled her nipples between them, my dick hardening more as she gasped and let out a throaty moan. I leaned forward, ready to suck them until she stopped me once again and climbed off.

"Don't leave," I whined.

"I'm not." She laughed again. "Open your eyes."

I wasted no time in opening them, immediately taking in the most gorgeous, perfect woman in front of me.

Her hair was down and curled in soft waves with makeup that brightened her eyes without being too much. But it was the red lipstick paired with the Mrs. Claus-looking lingerie that had my balls aching.

I knew that the bra portion was missing, but I couldn't have prepared myself for how incredible her tits looked propped up and on full display. The sheer fabric hugged her curves and gave me a glimpse of her wet pussy as she stepped to the side to open her legs for me.

"You look fucking amazing," I said, rubbing my thumb across the stubble on my jaw. "Fuck, Mak. I think you should wear this every day."

"I don't think the people of Sugarplum Falls would like that very much," she replied, wrinkling her nose.

"I didn't mean outside of this house," I corrected with a chuckle. "No one will *ever* see you like this. This lingerie is reserved for only me, just like your pussy."

"Well, then, in that case, I guess I should tell you that I bought more lingerie."

"That's the best news I've heard all day," I teased, immediately regretting it because knowing that her stalker was now behind bars was technically the best news I'd heard all year. "Now come over here so I can eat that pussy."

Her eyes widened slightly as a blush crept over her skin.

"I kinda thought I would give him some love first." She was bashful, and it was adorable, but there was no way I would be able to sit through a blow job knowing her pussy was that accessible and waiting for me.

"He can wait. Come here." I extended my hand to her,

watching as she nervously climbed up on the couch in her heels. "Sit on my face."

"What? Aiden, no! I don't want to smother you!"

"You won't. Now sit on my face."

"What if I fall?"

"I won't let you. Trust me."

She eyed me suspiciously as she accepted my hand and lined herself up against my face. Making sure she couldn't fall, I held her legs in place, still loving the heels she was wearing. Were they possibly going to poke holes in my couch from her standing on it? Possibly. Did I care? Not one bit.

I slid down and grabbed her hips to guide her until her pussy was lined up with my mouth. Then I wrapped my arms around the back of her thighs, holding her tightly as I swiped my tongue up her slit.

She gasped, and then I felt her fingers digging into my hair, pulling it as I licked her again and again. I loved this angle and being able to eat her easily with the crotchless panties. It was so fucking hot that my balls continued to ache, my cock begging for a release.

"Shit," she hissed, squirming against me the way she always does when she's close. "Aiden!"

I increased the pressure as I sucked her clit mercilessly, drawing every ounce of her orgasm out of her. Her body started to go limp as I helped her down and onto my lap.

"I fucking love these crotchless panties," I said, rubbing a finger along her pussy and smirking when she flinched from how sensitive she was.

"And I love this cock," she answered, leaning back slightly as she lined herself up over it, hovering as I pulled it out of my boxer briefs.

She gave me a wicked grin before sinking down slowly, her pussy warm and wet as it wrapped around my dick.

I closed my eyes and bit my lip, still not used to the intense sensation of being inside her without any protection.

"Open your eyes," she said softly, rubbing her hand across my jaw.

I did as she asked and found her watching me as she began riding my cock. Her hips swiveled in circles as she leaned back, allowing me full access to suck her nipples. I pulled one into my mouth, loving the way she moaned as she lowered a finger to rub her clit as she bounced harder.

I stood no chance of pacing myself with the image in front of me. Makayla was a force to be reckoned with on a good day, but her wearing this fucking lingerie as she fucked me was what destroyed me. I was on the verge of coming when she suddenly stopped and lifted herself off my cock.

Before I could ask what she was doing, she leaned over the side of the couch and put her ass up. I grinned as I climbed over and slid inside, loving how wet she was. Her pussy was tight as she gripped me, her ass bouncing as she met me thrust for thrust. I gripped her hips and gave it to her hard and deep, just the way she liked it.

I reached my hand down and rubbed her clit the way I knew she needed, grinning when I felt the first spasms as she cried out in pleasure. Her moan set me off as I shot ropes of hot cum deep inside her.

Thirty-Two

Makayla

"Merry Christmas," Aiden said as I rolled over and snuggled against his chest.

"Merry Christmas," I replied with a grin.

My body was sore and achy but in the best way. Last night with Aiden had started full of passion and ended early this morning with our final love making session.

"What time are you going to your mom's?"

"Around eleven. What time do you need to be at the bar?"

"Probably by four or five. I can let everyone know we're running a little late."

I lifted my face and looked at him, wondering how I got so lucky to wake up next to this perfect man on Christmas morning.

"I think we can make it on time. We'll have lunch around noon, then open presents after that."

"Sounds good."

"Are you sure you're still up for going with me?"

"Why wouldn't I be?"

"I don't know," I replied with a soft sigh. "I guess it just feels like the next big step, like when you meet your girlfriend's family for the first time. You already know my mom, but it would be the first time you're coming to Christmas dinner at her house."

"I think we've already established that we're in this for the long run, Mak. It doesn't bother me to spend the day with your family, and I'm happy that you want to come spend the evening at the bar with me."

"I think it's really cool that you host a Christmas dinner there every year."

"A lot of people don't have anyone to spend it with. I'd rather they be there to spend time with people who care about them than to be there so they can drink away their sorrows."

"You've always been such a great person with a big heart."

I shifted against him as my hand brushed against his dick. "Amongst other things," I teased, running my palm over the stiffening shaft before he pulled away.

"As much as I would love to fuck you right now, we gotta get up and get moving."

"For what?" I whined, not wanting to pass up sex with him.

"For one, we both need to shower. I don't need everyone knowing what we spent all night doing."

"I think this hickey you left me is pretty self-explanatory," I countered, pointing to the spot on my chest that I had no idea how I was going to hide today.

"You can wear a turtle neck."

"No way! I'll roast! Have you seen how hot my mom likes to keep her house? I was considering wearing that lingerie I showed you last night," I teased, watching as his eyes darkened and narrowed at me.

"Two, I have gifts I want you to open, and I'm highly impatient, so let's go."

He had already climbed out of bed but I refused to get up and rolled on my stomach instead.

"I'm not playing, Makayla," he warned, slapping my bare ass.

I pulled my lower lip between my teeth, trying not to get turned on right now.

"Alright, alright. I'm coming."

"Not now you're not. But you will tonight. Get dressed and meet me in the living room."

I didn't have a chance to say anything before he rushed out of the room, pulling his joggers up and tossing a shirt over his head on his way out. I shook my head, not bothering to hide the grin on my face. He was like a kid in a candy store and I loved his enthusiasm this morning.

When I walked into the living room, the curtains had been opened, displaying the fresh snow that had fallen overnight. The tree was lit up, and Christmas music played softly on the TV. I lifted my hands to my face and soaked it all in, not having had a Christmas like this in forever.

"Come sit down so I can start giving you your gifts," he said excitedly, guiding me to a spot on the floor by the tree.

I sat down and smiled at him as he started grabbing boxes

from beneath the tree. We still had some gifts here that I needed to take to my moms from the stuff I'd bought at Frosty Fest, plus the gifts we were taking to the bar tonight.

He started organizing boxes in a pile in front of me while I worked on digging out the gifts I had gotten him.

"They have numbers on them, so you know which to open first," he explained.

I arched an eyebrow at him, curious to see what he had gotten me. My gifts to him were all somewhat random and didn't need to be opened in any particular order.

"Um, I don't have any specific order for yours, so you can start wherever," I said with a slightly nervous laugh.

"Okay, but open yours first."

"Why don't we open them at the same time?"

"Mak…"

"Alright, alright," I said with a laugh. When he was determined, he was determined.

I picked up the box with the number one on it and tore the paper off. I could feel him watching me, and I hated the amount of attention that was on me right now. What if I didn't react the way he wanted me to?

Inside was a shirt box with a single piece of tape keeping it closed. I lifted it and peeked inside, my cheeks splitting as I pulled the scarf out.

"Oh my gosh! It's the scarf I fell in love with at Frosty Fest!"

"I know. I saw you looking at it, but when you didn't buy it, I made a note to go back and get it for you."

"Thank you, Aiden. That was so sweet of you."

"You're welcome."

His dimpled smile was distracting, but when he waved his hands for me to continue, I grabbed the next box. Inside was another shirt box, but this time, it had the purse I had fallen in love with from another vendor at Frosty Fest.

I held it up and hugged it, loving the way the soft leather felt. It was a mix of brown and pink with flower prints across it.

"I love it, thank you."

I continued opening the boxes and noticed that the first eight boxes all had items that I had admired at Frosty Fest but didn't buy.

"I can't believe you did all of this," I said, shaking my head. "Is that why you kept running off?"

He nodded, still grinning as he sat on the floor across from me with his presents still unopened.

"Yeah, I had to offer several free drinks to get them to hold the bags for me until I could go back later, so you didn't see them."

"You're such a goof," I replied with a laugh. "Thank you, though. This stuff is seriously amazing. I can't believe you memorized everything I touched and then went and bought it."

When I got to the next box, my heart started to race as I

pulled out a jewelry-sized box. I lifted my eyes to see if I could read anything on his face but he just stared at me with adoration as I finally opened the box.

Inside was the most beautiful bracelet I'd ever seen. It was rose gold bangles with a heart in the middle and a diamond centered inside the heart.

"Aiden!" I gasped, lifting it into the light and appreciating the beauty of it. "This is gorgeous!"

"I'm glad you like it. It was one thing you hadn't looked at, so I took a chance and hoped you would like it."

"I love it. It's so pretty." I immediately slid it onto my wrist as I continued to stare at it.

"There's one more," he said, nodding to the small box-shaped gift beside me.

I picked it up and unwrapped it, finding a snow globe inside. The scene was simple with a couple in the middle, kissing. I shook it, smiling when I saw the snow fall on them.

"I know that you have a life in LA and that you're worried about how things will be for us when you leave. So this is my way of reminding you that no matter what life throws at us or how shaken up we might get, we will always belong together, Mak."

My eyes filled with tears as I shook it again and watched the snow fall around them.

"It's perfect. Thank you," I said as I tried to keep from full on crying.

He scooted across the room and pulled me into his arms.

Thirty-Three
Aiden

Makayla had gotten me some awesome gifts, but my favorite was the skull whiskey set and the incredible bottle of whiskey that went with it. She'd told me how she'd searched high and low in town to find a decent bottle, then gone to the extreme of tipping one of her security guys a couple hundred bucks to go into the neighboring town to pick up this bottle when she found it online.

Lunch at her mom's had been fun and it made me miss having a family to spend the holidays with. Not that I regretted opening the bar every year to those who needed a place to go, but there was a difference between spending it with close friends and spending it with family.

Jill and Brock had done all of the cooking, and I couldn't help but notice how happy Jill was with him. Makayla noticed it as well and I caught her and her mom crying in the hallway as they talked about it. I knew that things had been hard for Mak as a kid when her mom divorced her dad when Makayla was in middle school. Jill never dated until recently, and it was like the universe waited until now to bring her the perfect partner to fulfill her life.

"Do you need help with that?" Makayla asked as I tried to balance the boxes of stuff I was carrying to the tables we'd set up for dinner.

It was always fun to see the bar set up for Christmas dinner because it never felt like a bar. With the lights turned up and the tables adorned with red linen tablecloths, it felt cozier. Add in the Christmas music and decorations, and it made it feel even more like home to me.

"I've got it, but thank you. You can grab the plates if you don't mind."

She nodded and grabbed the stack of disposable plates from the counter. Just because we made it feel cozy with linen tablecloths didn't mean I was in the mood to wash thirty-plus dishes. I was all about the easy button, which meant we kept things as simple as possible.

Soon people started showing up and the smell of food overwhelmed my senses, making me forget that I had just had lunch not that long ago.

"Where do you want the dessert?" Sam asked, holding up boxes from Sugarplum Sweets.

"I'll take those," Makayla offered, reaching her hands out before I swooped in and intercepted.

"I don't think so, you little fudge thief. These will go on that table until after dinner."

She stuck her lip out and pouted as Sam took his jacket off and hung it over one of the barstools.

I was thankful to have so many great friends to spend today with, but more importantly, to have Makayla there with me.

We sat down to eat once everyone arrived and the food was spread out on the table.

"I would like to take a moment before we eat to thank

everyone for being here today. A lot of us don't have somewhere to go for Christmas, and it warms my heart that you come here. We are the family that we make and choose for ourselves, and there's no better way to spend the holidays than to share them with the ones we love. Merry Christmas," I said, lifting my glass as everyone did the same.

Dishes were passed around the table as everyone began light conversations.

"Thanks for inviting us, Aiden. But I think next year, I'm going somewhere warm and tropical," Sam said. "Maybe Antigua."

"Antigua is nice this time of year," Makayla said, lifting a forkful of mashed potatoes to her lips.

"That's so awesome that you've traveled to so many places," Jasmin noted with a smile. "Do you have a favorite place you like to visit?"

Makayla shrugged as she set her fork down.

"I don't know. I think it depends on what I'm in the mood for. I love New York City and how fast-paced everything is. You can easily get lost in the crowd, which is nice when I'm wanting just to be me for a bit. I usually go when it's colder so I have an excuse to wear baggy clothes and hoodies so I can stay off people's radar. Plus, no one really questions it when they see someone wearing sunglasses in the middle of winter. They just go about their business, too busy to stop and question it."

We all laughed, but I felt this sharp pain of jealousy about the things Makayla had experienced while out living her life while I stayed in my small little bubble, living mine.

"I love Hawaii and try to escape to Kauai at least once a year. It's so calm there, and the views are breathtaking. Plus, I like to tour the north side of the island and pretend like I'm in Jurassic Park."

"Hey, maybe I'll do Christmas in Kauai next year instead," Sam said with a stupid grin. "I could totally get on board with dinosaurs."

"You know there aren't really dinosaurs there," Jasmin teased. "The only fossil you're likely to see is yourself."

"Hey now, you better watch it," he warned.

"So, are you planning to travel a lot next year?" Jasmin said, redirecting her attention to Makayla.

"I'm not sure how much personal traveling I'll be doing," Makayla said, glancing at me nervously. "But I go back on tour in February, so I'll be doing a lot of travel for that."

"That's so exciting! Is there anywhere on the tour you're most excited about?" Jasmin continued, leaning in with eyes wide and a smile plastered to her face.

"I'm excited to go to Japan. I've never been there before. That's a new stop on the tour next year. I'm also looking forward to being back in the UK. We had to add a few extra stops due to how quickly tickets sold out there, so I'll be spending more time there than anywhere else."

Sam started talking about where he would want to go if he were a famous musician and the tour he would do, but I tuned everyone out as the reality of everything sank in. Makayla had a life that didn't involve me, and if I loved her the way I claimed to, I couldn't stand in the way of it.

Thirty-Four
Makayla

Aiden was quiet on the way home from the bar, and I knew that it was because of the conversation at dinner about my going on tour. I wanted to assure him that it didn't matter, we would find a way to keep our relationship alive while I was gone, but I couldn't. I knew how insanely busy things were while I was on tour, and I didn't want to make promises to him that I couldn't keep.

By the time we got back to his place, I was exhausted. We grabbed our stuff from the truck and carried it inside, both ready to collapse on the couch when my cell phone started to ring.

"Hey, Curtis," I said, tucking my legs beneath me as I sat down.

"Hello, my favorite person in the whole entire world," he replied, making my eyebrows immediately arch.

"You're never this nice to me. What's wrong?"

I put the call on speakerphone when I noticed the concern on Aiden's face. Sean was already in jail, and unless I had another stalker I wasn't aware of, there was no need to be worried.

"I have some news."

"Like good news or bad news?"

"Both."

"Okay, you're killing me here. Just spill it already, please."

"Okay, so bad news first. Your upcoming world tour is being postponed. There have been some issues with the venues we booked in the UK as well as Tokyo, so we need more time to sort all of that out."

"What kind of issues?"

"Capacity issues. They assured us we would be able to book a certain amount at each venue, but now they're coming back, and those amounts are much smaller. So basically, we've oversold tickets because there isn't enough space to accommodate every ticket holder safely. We're back to square one with looking at new locations."

"You're kidding me. Those contracts were locked in place months ago. How are we just now finding out about it?"

"It seems the person we were working with was just arrested for embezzling and the person who stepped in to take over her job realized the issue and contacted me this morning."

"You shouldn't have to work on this stuff on *Christmas,*" I stressed, hating that I had spent the day with family and friends while my manager was sorting out business issues for me.

"It's not a big deal. I don't mind working on holidays. It's better than spending them with my mother, who wants to lecture me on all of my life choices."

"Okay," I said with a heavy sigh. "What's the good news?"

"The good news is that you're officially off for the next year. No tours lined up. When you get back to LA, I want to sit down and discuss the options for the world tour. If we're going to have to start over from scratch, I'd like to make sure we're doing things the way you'd like to. I also wanted to talk about doing a US tour since you haven't done one of those in a few years."

I worried my lip between my teeth as I felt Aiden stiffen beside me.

"I'm not coming back to LA," I blurted out, surprising myself as much as Aiden, whose head whipped around to look at me.

"I'm sorry, what?" Curtis asked with a hint of humor in his voice. "Did I hear you right that you're not coming back to LA?"

"You did," I said slowly, testing my words. "I'm actually moving to Sugarplum Falls."

I locked eyes with Aiden, tears filling mine as my nostrils burned as I tried to hold them back.

"I knew it. You went and fell in love, didn't you?" Curtis teased.

"No. I never fell out of it."

Thirty-Five
Aiden

I waited for Makayla to hang up her call with Curtis before attacking her with kisses as I wrapped her in my arms, determined to never let her go.

"Are you serious about what you just said?" I questioned, holding her body against mine as she sat on my lap.

She nodded and inhaled a shaky breath.

"Yeah. I think I am."

"You're really moving to Sugarplum Falls?"

"Is that okay?" she asked nervously, lifting her hand to her mouth to chew her nails.

I pushed her hand away and cupped her chin in my fingers as I forced her to look at me.

"Mak, there's nothing I want more in this world than to have you move here. Ideally, with me. In my house."

"Aiden," she said with a laugh. "I can't just move in with you."

"Why not? You're practically living with me already. It's literally just a matter of collecting your stuff from LA and putting it in my house."

Her brows furrowed slightly as she thought about it.

"Yeah, I guess you're right. Everything has felt so temporary that I didn't allow my mind to wrap around the idea that we were living together. It just kind of happened."

"Well, you had a stalker and needed a safe place to stay," I assured her. "But even with your stalker out of the picture, this will always be a safe place for you. This is home if you want it to be."

She grinned and leaned in to kiss me.

"I want this to be home."

I hugged her tighter, happiness overflowing from inside of me.

"I'll need to figure out the details of how to get everything moved out here, but that can wait until after the new year. And I'm sure I'll need to schedule time to go to LA so I can start recording new music."

"Why can't you do that here?"

"I don't have any equipment out here. I don't love the studio that I've been using, but Curtis was supposed to be looking into a new one."

"Can't we build you one here?"

"A professional recording studio?"

"Yeah. Why not?"

"I don't know where we would build one."

"I have space out back. I don't know how big of a studio you need, but I don't mind sacrificing the backyard to build you your own space back there. We can hire contractors to make sure everything is to your liking. But Mak, this could be really cool. And you wouldn't have to go back and forth to LA all the time."

"I do like the idea of having a studio here," she admitted with a smile. "I'll send Curtis an email and ask him to get started on this. He can get a team together and send them out to get started once we have an idea of what we want it to look like."

"Out of all of the Christmas gifts I've ever gotten, you staying in Sugarplum Falls is by far the best."

"Even better than the skull whiskey set?" she teased, giggling when I dug my fingers into her sides and tickled her.

Thirty-Six
Makayla

"When you said you wanted to get dressed up and go out to celebrate the New Year, I didn't think it would mean we would be spending it in LA," Aiden said, his hand rubbing the bare skin on my back where the dress dipped right above my ass.

"Well, since I needed to come pack up my things, I figured why not celebrate it here? Plus, you haven't been to LA before, so it's nice showing you around before I officially become a resident of Sugarplum Falls again."

The past week had flown by faster than I could have expected. Once I sent Curtis the email about wanting to set up a studio in Sugarplum Falls, he was on top of it. He'd hired a team, as well as an architect who sent over countless blueprints for me to go over until I found the one I loved. Unfortunately, they were all too big for the space Aiden had out back, but Hadley's aunt, Beth, found me the perfect spot in town. It helped to have someone who was a local realtor and knew the area so I could set up in a more quiet part of town.

I'd also signed new contracts for my world tour that would start in a year and a half. Curtis had handled all of my social media accounts, and part of us making it up to fans for moving the tour meant that the length of each show had been extended with the promise that I would be performing songs from my upcoming album that wouldn't be released until the tour started.

Things were moving fast but smoothly, reminding me why I paid Curtis what I did. He was more than just my manager. He was a godsend who handled everything for me so I could focus on the little things—like spending New Year's Eve with Aiden.

We'd gotten into LA the day before, and while it felt weird to go to my house, it wasn't as scary as I had imagined it to be because Aiden was there with me. I couldn't shake the feeling of being violated, knowing that Sean had been inside my house and gone through my belongings.

Curtis had also taken care of hiring a new person to manage my fan club. Thanks to my time in Sugarplum Falls, I recommended hiring Carissa, one of the sweet girls I'd met at Sugarplum Gifts. She was finishing high school and looking for a job while she decided what path to take in life. When she found out what happened with Sean, she assured me she was in a serious relationship with her boyfriend and promised she wouldn't fall in love with me or stalk me.

While I wanted to live a regular life in Sugarplum Falls, I knew that wasn't as realistic as I wanted it to be. I was still a well-known celebrity, and people came from all over the world to visit the cute little Christmas-obsessed town, which meant I had to keep my guard up for my own safety. It also meant that Tony and Patrick were now the newest residents of Sugarplum Falls.

"There's a bar on the corner we can go to if you'd like," I offered, leaning against Aiden's chest as we stared out the window, taking in the lights of LA. "Or, we can stay up here and watch the fireworks show when the clock strikes midnight."

"I think I'd rather stay here and devour you until the clock strikes midnight," he growled in my ear. "Show you a different kind of fireworks."

He slid his hand through the slit in my dress that went up to my thigh, caressing the skin as he kissed my neck.

My hair was up, giving him full access as his hand dipped into my panties and his fingers brushed my slit.

We'd gotten dressed up to go to dinner earlier, which was incredible. But I didn't want Aiden to feel cheated spending the rest of the night at the studio. I'd only brought him up here to show him the amazing view, but I wasn't about to complain about what was happening.

He bent down in front of me, his fingers grazing my skin as he removed my panties and slowly dragged them down my legs. Then he positioned himself in between my legs, shoving my dress to the side as much as he could as he began licking my clit.

I held onto the glass window, knowing no one could easily see what was happening with the lights off. My eyes fluttered closed as he gripped the backs of my thighs and held me steady as he sucked my clit.

Then, before I could come, he pulled away and wiped his mouth with the back of his hand before kissing me. I heard him unzip the zipper of his dress pants, then he stood behind me and lifted my dress. I was already wet and ready for him as he lined himself up at my entrance and slowly slid inside.

"Ahhh," I cried, loving the way he felt every time he entered me.

He used one hand to wrap around my waist to keep me steady while the other one slipped down to my pussy. He eagerly rubbed my clit, making me close to coming as he pounded into me from behind.

I tried to keep myself upright as my heels wobbled from the thrusting action. I placed my hands on the window, trusting it to hold my weight as I had the best sex I'd ever had in my entire life.

Aiden worked my clit faster as he drove into me harder.

"Shit," I cried out. "I'm coming!"

"Me too, baby," he grunted.

I felt the walls of my pussy spasm around him as fireworks lit up the sky in front of us. It was going to be a happy new year indeed.

****

Ready for more steamy holiday romance? Be sure to check these titles out:

Blame It On The Mistletoe
https://books2read.com/u/bw1rqe

Blame It On The Eggnog
https://books2read.com/u/38PPY6

Blame It On The Candy Canes
https://books2read.com/u/31DNo7

Blame It On The Blizzard
https://books2read.com/u/b6z6XE

Blame It On The Reindeer
https://books2read.com/u/baLAG6

Other Books By Samantha Baca

The Haven Brook Series
(small-town romantic suspense):

'Til Death Do Us Part (Haven Brook Book 1)

https://books2read.com/u/m2RJNR

The Cradle Will Fall (Haven Brook Book 2)

https://books2read.com/u/b6O0QE

The Ties That Bind (Haven Brook Book 3)

https://books2read.com/u/mqgoz8

A Very Haven Christmas (Haven Brook Book 4- Novella)

https://books2read.com/u/mvqGjj

Three Strikes, You're Gone (Haven Brook Book 5)

https://books2read.com/u/mvqL2z

The Dark Shadows Trilogy

(romantic suspense)

Five Steps Ahead (Dark Shadows Book 1)

https://books2read.com/u/38Q0gO

Ten Seconds Too Late (Dark Shadows Book 2)

https://books2read.com/u/3JRgVB

Against The Clock (Dark Shadows Book 3)

https://books2read.com/u/m2YwoR

The Stone Creek Series

(small-town- novellas)

Chocolate Covered Mistletoe (Stone Creek Book 1)

https://books2read.com/u/3LRk9N

Candy Coated Promises (Stone Creek Book 2)

https://books2read.com/u/mldP5Y

Pumpkin Spiced Possibilities (Stone Creek Book 3)

https://books2read.com/u/bojdwV

<u>Beaumont Creek Series</u>
<u>(small town)</u>

Just One Time (Beaumont Creek Book 1)

https://books2read.com/u/3G52zK

Second Chances (Beaumont Creek Book 2)

https://books2read.com/u/4Aj6Z0

Third Time's The Charm (Beaumont Creek Book 3)

https://books2read.com/u/b5lEyG

Four-ever Single (Beaumont Creek Book 4)

https://books2read.com/u/4j5jMX

Fifth Wheel (Beaumont Creek Book 5)

https://books2read.com/u/4XwKwa

<u>Whiskey Mountain Series</u>
<u>(small-town- novellas)</u>

Something To Talk About

https://books2read.com/u/4X62ag

Something To Think About

https://books2read.com/u/3GWAan

Something To Believe In

https://books2read.com/u/3yVzgB

Something To Live For

https://books2read.com/u/mllEOP

<u>Sugarplum Falls Series</u>
<u>(Holiday Novellas- can be read as standalone)</u>

Blame It On The Mistletoe
https://books2read.com/u/bw1rqe

Blame It On The Eggnog
https://books2read.com/u/38PPY6

Blame It On The Candy Canes
https://books2read.com/u/31DNo7

Blame It On The Blizzard
https://books2read.com/u/b6z6XE

Blame It On The Reindeer
https://books2read.com/u/baLAG6

Blame It On The Carols
https://books2read.com/u/me8E9z

Blame It On The Lattes
https://books2read.com/u/mB1E2A

Blame It On The Secret Santa
https://books2read.com/u/mY9dGY

<u>Standalone Books</u>

One Last Wish

https://books2read.com/u/mqg7D9

Finding Love In Apartment 2C (novella)

https://books2read.com/u/bze9aZ

Cocky Counsel: A Hero Club Novel

https://books2read.com/u/31Kzkn

All Is Fair In Food And War (novella)

https://books2read.com/u/bp8qjX

Holiday Books (novellas)

Snow Place To Go

https://books2read.com/u/4A560N

A Very Merry Kissmas

https://books2read.com/u/bPDgy7

A Christmas Wish

https://books2read.com/u/4EKXpE

Holiday Hijinks

https://books2read.com/u/4DP6Ze

Acknowledgments

How in the world have I written 34 books? Sometimes, it truly blows my mind when I look at how many stories I've created when, for so long it felt like I would never be able to complete one. I am a firm believer that things happen when the timing is right, and I'm thankful for the blessing I've been given to be able to do what I love.

None of this would be possible without some of the best supporters I have ever worked with. My alpha readers are not only amazing friends but also some of my biggest cheerleaders who push me when I need it and encourage me when this writing thing feels too hard sometimes. I'm so thankful for all of your help, and I truly believe I couldn't create the stories I do without your help. You ladies are one in a million! Thank you, Amanda, Azucena, Claire, and Valerie!

I'm also fortunate to have the most incredible beta readers! Malissa, Jackie, and Tamara—what would I do without you ladies? I mean, I seriously don't want to know because that would be a dark and depressing journey I would not want to go through. I'm so thankful for you taking the time to read my books and for giving me your honest feedback. You guys bring those final touches to the books that I love and appreciate!

I'd also like to give my thanks to Karrie, Cathy, and Anna for doing a quick readthrough to look for any last-minute things that we might have missed in the beta reads! Thank you for your help!

Since we're talking about my blessings and how lucky I am, I would like to thank the incredible ARC readers who chose to read this book early and help out by providing an honest review. You make such a difference in the book world, and whether people say it or not, your words help guide other readers on their journey when picking new books. Thank you for your help!

I also wouldn't be where I am today without the love and support of my readers. Some of you have been with me from the very beginning, and some of you are just now finding me. No matter where you found me on my journey, I'm so thankful you did. Thank you for giving my books a try. I truly hope you enjoy them!

My family kicks ass, and I couldn't do a lot of things without them. Thank you for your unwavering support and for continuing to brag to people about my books. I appreciate you all so much!

To my husband—you know how much I love and adore you. Thank you for everything you do for me and for allowing me to continue chasing my dream. I appreciate the sacrifices you make for your family and hope you know that they never go unnoticed. I love you so much. Thanks for being the inspiration for the swoony heroes I write about!

My girls—you have grown so much since I published my first book, and I love that your love for reading has flourished over the years. You guys are so supportive of my work, and I love how you tell everyone you know that your mommy is an author. It warms my heart to see you wanting to write your own books. I will always be here to help you along the way, whatever your dreams might be. I love you both so much!

About the Author

Samantha lives in the southwest with her husband and two small children after abandoning her childhood dream of living in a cabin in Colorado when she found that she couldn't afford to live there and was deathly allergic to the woods. When she's not writing, she's usually spouting off sarcastic remarks while drinking wine out of a coffee mug to look like a functional adult while chasing down her toddlers. She enjoys spending time with her family, watching reruns of Friends, and the 24/7 flow of coffee that can be found in her veins. Be sure to follow her on social media for updates on what she's working on.

You can find her here:

Facebook: https://www.facebook.com/AuthorSamanthaBaca

Instagram: https://instagram.com/author_samantha_baca

Goodreads: http://www.goodreads.com/authorsamanthabaca

Facebook Reader Group: https://www.facebook.com/groups/2945710968775398/

Webpage: www.samanthabaca.com

Newsletter: http://eepurl.com/g0NcSj

www.ingramcontent.com/pod-product-compliance
Lightning Source LLC
Chambersburg PA
CBHW031044310726
48969CB00007B/2107